PURSUIT OF THE OWL

Over a dozen nations line up for the longest and most gruelling contest on earth—a non-stop yacht race around the world. But not all the crews and skippers are dedicated to winning. Against a wild background of terrifying storms, massive seas, killer whales, sharks and Cape Horn even bigger dangers lurk above and beneath the waves. A beautiful girl—locked for months with beefy sailors—finds that not all the sharks are in the water . . . The race between the sporting giants of the world becomes a shuddering contest between men on land, but still some yachts manage to finish unscathed. Despite a final cruel twist at the end of the circumnavigation, one boat manages to win . . . but it doesn't finish there.

Pursuit Of The Owl

by

ANTHONY HOWLETT

ROBERT HALE · LONDON

ISBN 0 7091 9507 9

Robert Hale Limited
Clerkenwell House
Clerkenwell Green
London EC1R 0HT

Photoset by Art Photoset Limited.
Printed in Great Britain by
St Edmundsbury Press, Bury St Edmunds, Suffolk.
Bound by Hunter & Foulis Ltd.

ONE

Fog. Thick, grey impenetrable fog. It hung over the ribbon of autobahn linking Berlin and the Polish port of Stettin like an unmoving cloud of evil. Helmut Keller checked the fuel gauge. Wismar, on the Baltic coast, seemed a long way away. He pushed his foot down on the accelerator as far as he dared and concentrated hard on the line of the sunken kerb flickering past in the diffused dipped beam. It would soon be dark . . . and then it would be worse.

Keller drew on his American cigarette, stifling the reflex cough which rasped from his lungs as the smoke scorched deep into them. He glanced nervously at his watch and settled back uneasily in the seat, intent on the road and the long journey. At least the fog would hide him as he travelled.

The monotony of it all ate into him, while kilometre on kilometre drifted past, mesmerising him in the unreal gloom. It seemed to Keller it was a great irony that he should be heading away from Berlin, away from the Wall and away from the escape routes to the West that he and the others had painstakingly built up over the years. Now it was *his* turn . . . but he was heading the other way. Away!

With the hottest set of documents that the West was ever likely to see. He smiled to himself. If it came off, it would be spectacular. Mentally he ticked off, yet again, the check-list of the contents of his small black case, then he worked his mind over everything once more, feeling the beads of nervous sweat pimple up on his square forehead. His hands were clammy on the wheel. He cursed himself. Too nervous, he told himself. You're too nervous. What had he missed? Suppose he had forgotten something vital . . .

Many kilometres away, also heading for Wismar and also nervous, butterflies tormenting his stomach and bowels, was Hans Mann, an officer in the East German army and now, thankfully, able to forget the intense course he'd been on, a course in which, bored and mechanical, he'd soaked up the latest techniques of Warsaw Pact anti-tank weaponry. His nervousness had nothing to do with military matters, however, but with the greatest adventure that he could contemplate in life, something that would realise all the dreams he'd ever had . . . crew member in *Der Rote Vogel*, taking part in the greatest sail race the world had ever known, the first non-stop round-the-world battle between the yachts of nations competing as nations. *Der Rote Vogel*—the Red Bird—was East Germany's entry. And he, Hans Mann, was going to be a part of her! He wondered again how he'd manage in the huge seas of the Southern Ocean, way beyond the Atlantic which was the limit of his sailing experience. Cape Horn! The empty nervousness rolled round his stomach as he fidgeted, lurching to his feet to make his way along the train carriage. When he returned, he sank into a fitful sleep, the train bumping along slowly in the fog.

But for Keller, driving faster now as the fog lifted, there would be no sleep on this particular night. The warmth gradually permeated the saloon and crept into his stiff limbs as he turned up the heater. Keller wondered how the others were getting on, taking their decoys through the old routes which even now might still be quite safe. It made him angry, when he remembered the three years it took him to build them up, to think of that bastard Braun. There had never been any real proof that he'd taken the route plans over to the other side, but Keller was glad that if anybody had to eliminate him it was he who was chosen. Now it made him angry again. If it hadn't been for Braun this would have all been quick and straightforward. Now it was complicated and risky. But daring! That was the only thing that appealed to him.

He was suddenly alert. He saw the glow of the lights looming over the border control between East Germany and Poland. Ice cool now, he stiffened and drove through the approaches and the soldiers guarding the border point. There were no difficulties.

Keller breathed more easily now. He left the autobahn, skirted to the right of Stettin, checked carefully behind and was grateful for the lingering mirk of the fog, looking for the thick copse where the big, dripping, black trunks of twisted oaks would hide the car until he was away. That was safe enough. There would be no risk of the authorities finding their way through all the forged documents, plates and numbers in the vehicle.

He found the wood, parked and then pointed his long,

olivine face towards Stettin. He walked briskly, carrying the black valise easily. Three kilometres from the car he threw the keys away and headed for the railway station.

Before he chose his carriage he walked along the train until, through the unwashed glass, he saw the man who would provide, unknowingly, the first step in his journey back to London. Keller boarded the train and sat down opposite Mann who, alone in his suppressed excitement, was sleeping deeply.

Keller watched the injection take effect. Mann's eyes flickered at him. In that tiny moment the two men looked deeply inside each other. Keller felt no pity. He watched the slow squirm of Mann's death, glanced around to satisfy himself that he was not being watched himself, and then, with quick efficiency, searched the body, extracting from the pockets all evidence of identification and slipping substitute papers into Mann's clothes. The documents would, at the very least, take the police on a false trail for long enough, so that he could continue his planned escape with success. Keller took several long breaths before carrying on. He switched cases. He gave Mann the small black valise, which now included more false information, and then he took over Mann's canvas case. He opened the zips and transferred into it the documents which he had brought with him from Berlin.

Keller was six feet two and strong as an ox. Without effort, and hoping that he would not have to explain to anybody his friend's "sudden illness" which necessitated fresh air, he quickly hauled Mann to his feet, slung his limp arm around his own neck, supported Mann around the waist with one hand and, the black case in the other hand, walked with the dead man out of the carriage to the exit door. It took only a few seconds to release the catch against a roar of whirling, buffeting wind and, in the sudden clatter, to drop Mann and the case into the racing darkness.

The train slipped on.

Keller strode quietly back to his seat. He was still alone. He closed his eyes and slept soundly until the train reached Rostock. Later that day Helmut Keller, alias Hans Mann, stepped onto the deck of *Der Rote Vogel* presenting himself to the skipper, a diminutive man with a big hooked nose which, at that moment, was drooping into an open hatch in the coachroof. He extended his hand.

"I'm Hans Mann."

"Steinhoff," grunted the small man. "Sorry to call you here at such short notice but Müller broke his back. For no good reason, he fell from the bosun's chair while checking the rigging at the masthead. He will live." He looked back into the hatch and added, "As a cripple."

Keller pointed to his case. "Where can I put this so I can get started? Is there much left to do?"

Steinhoff drew himself up to his five feet four inches. "Your bunk, when it is not occupied by Blenken on the opposite watch, is the second one along on the port side. He will tell you where to put your gear. We are waiting for two spinnakers to arrive and then we can go. We are expecting them today or tomorrow." He surveyed Keller. "I hope you are not clumsy, too. I have no room on my ship for clumsy men."

"You will find me as lithe as a sea maiden," smiled Keller, with easy familiarity which he hoped would infect the other man. "But I'm strong, too. You won't find me lacking, as long as the grog's good."

Steinhoff looked at him sternly. "You will have no alcohol on board my yacht," he snapped. He watched Keller's face fall, and then laughed. "At least, not until we're round the Horn." He slapped Keller on the shoulder and turned away to push his hooked nose back down the hatch, squeezing his arm down it to make a mysterious adjustment.

Keller, a sailor of sorts for most of his life, swept his eye over the clean lines of the 77 ft. *Rote Vogel*, her flat decks, with nothing to smash under the onslaught of the seas she might expect in the 27,000-mile battle of endurance, and her deep cockpit, housing only the wheel at the moment. Fourteen crew would be sailing the big sloop, her single mast pointing commandingly into the sun. "Hopefully they will continue without me after London," he thought, chatting with Blenken while he stowed his kit.

"How long will it take us to get to the Thames?" Keller asked.

"Depends on the wind," replied Blenken, looking up with a surprise which immediately made Keller resolve to watch his mouth. "If we can get away today or tomorrow we hope to be in time for the Worldsail reception at Tower Bridge two nights before the start. A big fleet of sightseers is already arriving in the Thames Estuary to see us off."

"I'm sorry," said Keller quickly. "Nobody has told me much. It's been a bit of a rush."

He planned to slip into London when they berthed there, and not to return to the yacht. He envied the crew. But he had to complete the job.

Keller was beginning to worry about the delay. He sensed an anxiety in the whole crew that they would not get away from Wismar on time. "What happens if we don't get away today or tomorrow?"

The longer they remained in the port the more chance there was that he might be detected. And the longer they remained here, even if he remained undetected, the chances of his getting ashore in London according to plan became slimmer.

Blenken opened his hands and ran them through his greasy hair. "We have discussed this very carefully. To have a chance of winning the race we need those big spinnakers. If we have not got them we stand no chance at all, because all the other boats will have them. We can still have a chance of winning, even if we have to wait for the sails to arrive and we are late for the start. But we hope that won't happen."

Keller remained cool. "Are we allowed to start late?"

"Oh yes. The British Royal Ocean Yacht Club is laying a start line in the North Sea, opposite the mouth of the Thames. If we miss the actual start we just cross the line later—and we'll probably catch up with everyone else in the Channel."

"You'll let London know by radio, I suppose."

"That's right. The rules say we must carry at least one, to report our positions at intervals. And, of course, to help out in emergencies." Blenken lay down on his bunk and waved Keller into the bunk above him. "But we do not expect any disasters. We have been training together. If you look in the aft cabin, which we are calling the wardroom, you'll see that the watch rotas, duties and so on have all been worked out. The sails, rigging and gear are all straightforward. You'll have no difficulty as long as you mix in."

On the other side of the North Sea in London the big, lonely frame of Commander Tom Nelson was etched against the mast-spiked backcloth of St. Katherine's Dock. One step away from his yellow-booted feet on the edge of the quay-heading was the teak-laid deck of his latest command. He shrugged his wide shoulders at the seventy feet of yacht bought at the last minute for the British Combined Services Crew by London's new newspaper, the Tribune. Well, at least Britain had a boat in the race—but his shrug mirrored his resignation at the suddenness thrusting him to the head of a dangerously small and untrained crew. Nelson—veteran of two trans-Atlantic singlehanders—was not happy. Nearby were the American Eagle and the Russian Vladimir, slick boats with slick crews and slick gear. The British wouldn't stand a chance!

Within an hour he had the crew on board—Pete "Sparky" Campbell on the radio, Geoff Howard, John Tooke, Bob "Sixpence" Tanner and a huge bearded man grunting to the name of Bob Le Strange. He was the cook. Pete Good was navigator. The day before, the only other member of the crew—Sally Downes—had arrived, to their delight, but Nelson was far from delighted. A short-handed crew, a raw girl and no preparation for any of them gave him no hope for a race which might take 140 days.

Together they did what they could during two days of concentrated work before heading out for the start in the company of 13 other boats. Only *Der Rote Vogel* was missing.

"Where is she?" Nelson asked, before they left.

"She'll be here," replied Eric Pritchard, race committee secretary. "But probably a bit late. She radioed a couple of hours ago. She still has a long way to come and the wind is light and heading her. Had to hang on for some extra sails. Damned nuisance, but it won't spoil the start. Everyone else is here . . . and there are hundreds of small boats of every description ready to see the race off. We've never made a start from this area before, but we wanted this grand occasion in London. And I think it's paid off, don't you?"

Nelson grunted without commitment.

Pritchard nodded over towards a boisterous knot of people. "I see the Yanks have cornered your new Sally Downes. Bloody attractive girl, isn't she? Wouldn't mind being locked up with her for 27,000 miles myself."

Nelson ignored him and cast his eye over the opposition . . . Eagle, Vladimir, France's La Bohème, White Nile from Australia, Saint Mark from Italy, Turkey's Dream Bagger, Excelsior entered by a consortium of small states calling themselves African Unity, a boat with no name from Uganda, the Royal David from Israel, Pretty Flamingo from Brazil, Wily Robin from Saudi Arabia, Canada's Living Doll, and the Otto from West Germany.

He smiled ruefully at the name chosen for the British contender. The Hood.

The start was off the Thames estuary in an area free from the treacherous sandbanks which have lured sailors to their deaths for centuries. One end of the line was marked by the Royal Navy frigate, HMS Norfolk, being used by the Royal Ocean Racing Club for their committee boat, bearing an old cannon to fire the series of starting guns. The other end of the mile-long line was marked by an anchored passenger ferry, chartered from Felixstowe by the Tribune for honoured guests and those members of the Press who would not be in the huge flotilla which even now was prepared to see off the racing fleet.

Nelson cocked his head at the blustery wind, which flecked the grey waves with spray as it gusted. He felt a shudder within himself as he looked at the hundreds of small boats ploughing and heeling and rolling and bobbing, sighing and spuming. All too close, he said to himself. They're all too close in this breeze.

Helmut Keller clicked his teeth in impatience as he donned his yellow oilskins. If he couldn't get ashore he would have to change his plans. For a brief second he gazed at the white plastic shells containing the self-inflating liferafts lashed to the coachroof. He just as quickly dismissed the idea of using one to get into the sea and onwards to the shore. There would be too many crew on deck. Besides, there was another reason why he shrugged the idea from his mind. He could not swim.

Keller climbed out into the cockpit and felt the shock of cold air. The Red Bird's sharp bow sliced through the cold water with an urgency to match Keller's. He lurched to the foredeck, where the crew was about to hoist a bigger jib in an effort to increase speed. Keller felt an icy chill of apprehension.

Off the Thames the wind blustered over the heeled fleet, surging the boats forward under a mass of sails. Nelson looked again at the cauldron of little craft tagging along with the racing yachts. "At the moment I'm more frightened of them," he said, cocking his thumb at the accompanying flotilla, "than I am of the Roaring Forties. They just don't seem to know how dangerous this is." He stabbed his finger in anger at a small outboard launch wallowing in their path with its engine stopped and a man crouched over the stern tugging at the starter in a desperate attempt to get it going. Howard moved the wheel quickly to starboard to avoid the little boat. He looked cool. Nelson's grim eyes met the frightened glance of the man in the launch. Fool! Hadn't boats like the Hood got enough to contend with without idiots setting out onto the sea unable to make sure their bloody boats would go? Nelson and Howard glanced at each other in relief.

"Better keep a good look-out," advised Nelson. "With all those boats and fools about it could get dodgy." He glanced nervously at his watch and then scanned the grey horizon. "I can't see anything yet." He raised his glasses and looked again. "Nothing." He called down to Good. "Are we anywhere near the line yet, Pete? It's like bloody Picadilly Circus out here."

"Not yet. Should see something in about thirty minutes." Good lurched over the chart table and hung on as the Hood heeled sharply.

Nelson made his way below to Campbell, who was listening intently in his headphones. He tapped his shoulder.

Campbell turned and took off the 'phones.

"Is it fixed?" Nelson asked, without anxiety.

"Yep. Good as gold now. I've just picked up a message from the Red Bird. They're going to be late for the Big Off."

Nelson shrugged. "I'm beginning to wish we had planned to be late, too. It's chaos out there. I've never seen so many boats in my life. I bet even Dunkirk seemed quiet compared with this lot."

In less than three hours, with HMS Norfolk well in sight, the Hood was heading south-east, sweeping down towards the start line through the fleet of sightseers and waving well-wishers.

"I don't like it," murmured Nelson. "We'll find it difficult to manoeuvre in this cram." As he spoke he saw the white puff he had been waiting for shoot from the cannon on the Norfolk and signal the breaking out of the race flag. Ten minutes to go. There was a brief delay before the crack from the gun hit them. Nelson looked around, his determined urge to compete without concessions over-coming the sick nervousness deep within him.

La Bohème was creaming along less than a hundred yards away. Beyond her was the Italian boat, Saint Mark. Between the Hood and the French craft were two small yachts and a speedboat. There were more behind on the port side. Ahead a little way were three of the racing fleet, separated from each other by only a few yards . . . the Australian White Nile, the Excelsior and the Ugandans, powering together through the greyness, slicing through the milling boats . . .

The disaster was brief and comprehensive.

A small, lumbering cruising yacht, white and anaemic,

was dithering as the three starboard racing yachts bore down on her. She had been attempting to cut across their bows, but suddenly thought better of it. Now, in the panic of turning, she lost the wind and wallowed without either direction or power. The bright red hull of the Ugandans luffed up suddenly towards the wind in her attempt to take avoiding action, but was herself baulked to port by the green Excelsior. The Ugandan yacht crashed into her, bouncing off and cleaving right through the white boat. She luffed again, her port bow stove in and splintered, tearing into Excelsior once more with a shattering blow, the African Unity yacht herself now in difficulties, coming up into the wind and slicing into the White Nile with a rending crash, the two boats locking together, their masts and rigging tangled and snapped in a death dance.

The Hood was in trouble, too, unable to avoid the melée and clipping the stern of the Ugandan boat with a judder.

In a minute it was all over. Two yachts lay rolling peacefully in a mass of wire rigging; quiet now, as if they had had their passionate orgasm and now breathed contentedly in each other's arms. The stunned, holed Ugandans were sinking slowly. Nearby, the débris that once had been the small white yacht rose and fell with the heavy swell, two limp bodies in buoyancy jackets floating silently in the wreckage.

The Hood surged on with a hole in the bow above the water line, Nelson lying anxiously along one of the forward bunks, his head in the hatch of the chain locker in the bow inspecting the damage. He lifted himself up. "It could be a lot worse. The hole is about a foot above the water line and at the moment there's only spray coming in. For the time being we can patch it with ply on both sides but once we reach warm weather we can repair it properly with the GRP repair kit. For the time being we'll just stuff the hole with anything to stop water getting inside."

They crossed the line first—a split-second after the starting gun . . . alone now, some distance from the mess of craft converging on the boats kicking in their death throes behind.

Campbell radioed to tell the race committee that the Hood was carrying on. The radio crackled in reply: "You're lucky. The Ugandans are out. And it looks as if African Unity and the Aussies are out as well. Good luck. Over."

Seventy miles away, as the Red Bird bucked into short, steep seas, Keller gritted his teeth. The decision was final. They would not put into London. The Red Bird would cross the line for the start after the rest had gone, and sail on. On round the world.

The chaos at the start had spurred on the East German crew, for by the time the mess had been sorted out they would not be too far behind the rest. They tightened the sheets and heeled to the challenge.

Keller winched in the jib sheet against the ratchet and calmly looked at his skipper. "I think we shall win."

TWO

The wind dropped as the depleted racing fleet, stripped of the parasitical craft following them out of the Thames, strode into the Channel and into the busy shipping lanes which would mean constant look-out day and night until they were out of the western end, across the Bay of Biscay and into the Atlantic.

Nelson welcomed the relative peace in which the Hood could make her temporary repairs. It meant nothing that she was ahead. All the other yachts except the Red Bird, which was many miles behind but already over the start line, were in sight.

Le Strange—burly and flamboyant, with a slightly flattened nose from some brawl in the past—was hanging over the bow with his feet knotted into a rope held by Campbell and Howard, drilling and bolting through the outside ply patch while Sally tightened the nuts on the inside of the interior patch.

Nelson, lightly holding the wheel to keep the Hood on course, watched with satisfaction. Perhaps he'd misjudged this crew. They'd come through the first emergency well and that put him in better frame of mind to contemplate the

huge seas and storms which would drive them on
mercilessly in the big oceans of the world. He smiled at the
antics of Le Strange over the bow. Le Strange was a man
he'd already warmed to. Efficient. Resourceful. Bouncy.
The kind of man to keep up morale when the crew was
down. The kind of man who could be relied upon in the
shit-or-bust danger of the southern seas. The kind of man
who'd be trying to screw the arse off Sally Downes . . .

He glanced lustfully through the length of the boat to
Sally's rounded bottom, curving tightly within her faded
blue jeans while she wriggled in the bow with the spanner.

Tooke, smaller than Le Strange but sporting the same
kind of dark beard, came up to his side. "Fantastic," he
enthused. "Absobloodylutely fantastic!" He twitched at
the Nikon camera round his neck. "I got shots all the way
through that mayhem. If we do a book afterwards it'll be
fantastic. All colour." Tooke glanced down the hatchway
and saw Sally's bottom trying to get out of the jeans. "Hey,
look at that!" He leapt down below with shutter cocked.
She swore at him. Nelson grinned.

The repair done, the Hood was soon under full sail once
more, a steady breeze blowing from the Continent, giving
the fleet a pleasant beam wind the whole length of the
Channel, taking the dozen boats, including the sparkling
Red Bird which had caught up now, through the strong
tides, past the Needles, past Brittany and the Channel
Islands, out of the western end of the Channel and into
Biscay, where a new kind of rolling swell thrust itself
constantly up against the rounded bilge of the Hood.

Six days after the start the Red Bird took the lead.
Nelson scanned her through his binoculars, studying her

with professional envy. The hiss of the boat through the Biscay swell stirred him. He looked up at the straining white of the main, at the big genoa pulling easily at the bow, and down at the clean, easy lines of the Hood and turned away from the Red Bird to the real worry—a distant smudge of dirty weather. Waiting ahead was the tail end of Hurricane Freda, into which they were heading at a brisk pace. The Hood prepared . . . with apprehension.

It was not long before the first ragged heralds of the storm brushed over the Hood, digging her down into the sea and then impatiently flinging the water off in stinging sheets of spray and white anger. The mainsail was reefed down. A small, tough storm jib was set, enough to keep driving the boat forward, and the Hood lurched to meet her new adversary.

It was the noise which got to Keller most. He lay on his bunk holding himself in tightly. Only Blenken was in the cockpit with Steinhoff, who was at the helm. The Red Bird crashed through the ferocious breaking seas with a noisy venom, lurching, pitching, tossing . . . The moment Keller had been dreading had arrived. The moment of nausea. Sea-sickness. He had already begun to sweat profusely and felt his bowels churn. It welled up within him like a waking volcano, sweeping over him in a blind, green wave until he had to race from his bunk up to the cockpit.

Steinhoff forbade him to go on deck unless he wore his storm gear and harness.

"But . . . but . . . I must . . . sick." Keller spluttered as the vomit welled up. Involuntarily he threw it forward into the cockpit, heaving, grunting and vomiting again. Steinhoff roared with laughter. Keller painfully retched once more.

"Don't worry. The next big sea will wash away your shame," cried Steinhoff, as he pushed the wheel to meet the next thundering wave. The sea came, creaming over the coaming into the self-draining cockpit, swishing around the foot of the washboards which prevented water going below. Steinhoff and the Red Bird ploughed on together, a roaring, laughing couple holding hands in a romp through the storm as if all it held was a commanding joy instead of the dangerous, all-consuming fire of an omnipotent mistress of all that she surveyed. Keller looked down, holding on weakly. The cockpit sole was clean, washed contemptuously by that single sluice. The yacht lurched over again, throwing Keller down to the cabin floor. He crawled back to his bunk and tried to die.

It lasted all that day, through the fierce night and all the next day. But as a new evening fell the wind hinted that it might drop, too. The Hood was crashing her way through violent seas, Tanner at the helm, shining wetly in the gathering gloom, eyes half shut against the icy spume clouding every inch of the whining air . . . solid as a stinging sheet.

They held on grimly at every second's shuddering collision with the next mad wall of water.

Nelson grabbed at the chart table to steady himself as the Hood hit a bigger wave. As always, they felt the yacht lower herself into the shuddering trough, sensed her feel the weight of water bouncing into her, felt her hold there and, always with relief, felt her rise again. Always she rose again . . .

By morning the wind had gone, leaving in its wake a confused sea thundering out its subsiding anger in all directions and a calm which frustrated the Hood. Like the other yachts, which had been scattered by the ferocity of the tattered remains of Hurricane Freda, she was impatient. The storm had halted their forward drive out towards the Atlantic past Madeira and the Canaries and on towards the Cape Verde Islands perched way out in the ocean off the westerly rounded buttock of Africa. Now they all wanted to hoist up their bibs and go.

Nelson was as impatient as the boat. The East Germans were now way ahead, flying along while the Hood was being held back by a more fickle breeze. Nelson ordered the crew to prepare to hoist the genoa and full main to gather into Hood's skirts the regular north-east trades which, when they arrived, would take the fleet down, down, down into the rainy region of calms and squalls . . . the Doldrums, where places in the race could change by hundreds of miles depending on which yacht found a little bit of private wind. Nelson wanted to win. Already the Red Bird was perhaps 70 or 80 miles in the lead. The Hood was probably second, although nothing had been heard yet of the Italians, who were thought to be up somewhere among the leaders. America and Russia, who looked as if they were going to hang on to each other's apron strings right round the world, were behind, just over the horizon, out of sight but a constant threat.

The Red Bird and her crew, urged on by the reckless confidence of Steinhoff, were in high spirits. Except Keller.

He felt—and was—totally trapped. It seemed slightly ridiculous that when he should be in London handing over highly valuable information, he should, instead, find himself in the middle of the Atlantic with thousands of miles of sailing, storms, sickness and other hazards in front of him. He had to get on shore. There must be a way somehow. And once on land he'd find a way to England. He'd used his wits like that before. All he needed was terra firma underneath his feet and he'd be away. But that was the problem. How to reach land?

The fleet had now sailed through the eastern entrance to the Atlantic. Once past Madeira and the Canaries, travelling down the west coast of Africa, they would be in the sunshine of the north-east trades—winds which should blow them into the Doldrums and their mixture of stillness, mists, sudden squalls and heavy rain. Here they would pray for the squalls to carry them out of the frustration into the south-east trades and then deep into the South Atlantic, where a big area of high pressure lurked constantly at that time of year like a big albatross wheeling around the waves which curl towards Cape Town on the tongue tip of southern Africa. The skippers would win or lose by their luck in predicting where the calm winds of the High would be and which course they would take to pick up the gales and winds blowing around it.

Keller was biting his lip. If the Red Bird went straight down the middle of the Atlantic he was in trouble for a few more thousand miles. The South African navy was stationing a ship a hundred miles off the southern tip of Africa . . . the

Cape marker which the fleet would have to round before the roller-coaster ride through the Roaring Forties, the huge waves rolling westwards virtually unchecked around the world at latitude forty degrees south, skirting the icebergs hanging on the chest of the Antarctic. If they made it across there safely, the navigators of the fleet would be sorely tested, for a precision landfall would be needed to take the yachts to a marker between the northern and southern islands of New Zealand.

Keller felt his spirits sinking. If he could not get ashore now he would probably not get a chance until New Zealand. After New Zealand it was the rolling South Pacific, horrendous Cape Horn and back up the Atlantic to a marker off Florida and Bermuda before crossing the North Atlantic to the finishing line off Portsmouth.

Keller shrugged. It had to be North Africa or he was stuck on board for the rest of the race. It worried him. How long before his identity was in question? How long before Hans Mann would be identified back home and the message radioed to *Der Rote Vogel*? Nervously he fingered his wide belt. It was hollow, tough canvas folded over and stitched so that documents would be hidden there. Keller had wrapped his papers in self-sealing polythene bags first.

That was more like it! The Hood was flying along, surfing down the face of the regular waves passing beneath her like giant prehistoric beasts. Nelson was at the helm, feeling the hard tug at the wheel at each surge and then holding the Hood there against the fierce pressure on the helm to keep her creaming on in a welter of flying spray and the roar of foam flung aside by the sharp impatience of the bow. He laughed aloud, just as Steinhoff would have done. This was what he had come for! He glanced up at the sun and felt the warmth on his cheek.

He wondered where the Red Bird was. These were early days to think about winning or losing, but he knew now that the Hood could do it if she kept her sails up and the cream of foam bundling past in that sluicing hiss of surf and speed.

He planned to avoid the High by going as close as he dared into the African shore, a plan being decided on, too, by the Red Bird about 50 miles ahead.

Good considered the proposal and brightened. "The Italians have had to pull into Spain with a buckled boom. Courtesy of Freda. So we won't have to worry about them—at least not for a while. That delay will take some catching up."

"It depends," said Nelson. "It depends on whether you're right about the course you've set. You can lose a hundred or more miles a day in the Doldrums if you're wrong. Lose that much for five days and you could end up at the back of the fleet."

Good nodded slowly. "I know. I said it was a risk. Anyway, there's no chance of a calm for a while. The glass has begun to drop and I wouldn't mind betting we're in for some dirty."

Nelson ignored him, drinking in the warmth and the sunshine and the rolling decks as the Hood sliced her hissing way southwards, on to the Cape of Good Hope, on to the Indian Ocean, on to Cape Horn. He breathed in contentedly, smiling as he took the mug of lemon tea from Tanner.

"Thanks," said Nelson. He sipped it. "How'd you know I like lemon tea?"

"Sally said."

Nelson raised an eyebrow.

Tanner laughed. "Le Strange is trying to get his leg over there. He's having a bit of a job, though."

Nelson checked the helm. "She seems a bit of a tough bird. Tries so hard to be on a level with the rest of us she forgets she's a woman . . . with nice tits, a firm bum and . . and . . ."

"Don't remind me." Tanner laughed again and Nelson laughed with him. But as he did so he felt another hardening gust grab the Hood and bury her head into the sea, heralding a wild four hours. The wind rose slowly, gathering itself, like a malevolent giant bunching his muscles before striking out indiscriminately. It was not long before the gale howling through the rigging and the sound of the sea whipping against the clean hull of the Hood joined together in a crashing fury, rising in a mad crescendo.

The Hood ploughed on, undaunted by the spuming white foam hurtling by wetly and then rising up into the air so that every breath inhaled salt and water. Rising. Falling. Lurching. Lurching. Crashing through the seas with a defiance which shook her to the frames and bulkheads.

The crew, apart from Campbell, taking his stint at the helm, and Tooke, who was continuing to batten things down on top, sat in silence, listening with their own private fears to the water smashing past that thin skin of glass fibre. feeling the Hood mounting and falling in the immense seas. feeling the yacht heel and duck as the blows of nature swept over her. It was violent, but although it was brief it left a legacy which was to haunt them for the rest of the race.

"Not a peep!" called Campbell. "The radio's gone. It's U-S."

The aerial on the masthead had gone, swept away by one of the green-water waves which had hit the Hood during the height of the storm. A makeshift aerial was raised but the radio remained mute apart from desperate crackles and strange whines.

Good was thoughtful. "We should pass pretty close to the Cape marker. Can't we get a message over that the radio is on the blink and we need a replacement?"

"If we do that," answered Nelson, shaking his head, "we can say goodbye to the race. The rules say that we're not allowed to take on new or replaced equipment. The Italians will be put out by that rule unless, at the end of the race, they can argue their case to the committee with any degree of success."

By now they were drifting, sails banging backwards and forwards by the motion of the sea without any wind. But the sun was shining again, pouring its heat upon them and transforming the sea into a sheet of blue sparkle, heaving its jewels to and fro.

But they were not alone. Howard nodded towards the horizon, where a minute dot was barely discernible many miles away. Nelson raised his binoculars and studied the horizon for a few minutes before handing Geoff Howard the glasses. "I reckon that, sir, is *Der Rote Vogel*. What d'you think?"

Howard raised the glasses. "Could be right. But have you noticed? There's no jib up."

Nelson took the binoculars. "Perhaps they're in the middle of changing sails. They might have found a wind."

But all was not well on *Der Rote Vogel*. Steinhoff examined the rigging. The forestay bottle-screw was badly damaged. The mast could have come down had not the crewman who made the discovery kept his head and got the sails down.

Steinhoff and Bauer ordered a replacement and exchanged glances. Keller watched in dismay.

The deep indigo of evening was giving way to night itself. Nelson, hardly daring to breathe for fear that he might break the magic spell, leant on the aft rails. He watched a hammerhead shark drifting twenty yards from the boat, sensed the evil there rippling the water, and shuddered. But he wished the moment would never end. In one direction the sky was blue-black. In the other it was deep flame, a fire of joy which died rapidly, changing to brown and then black. The air carried merely the slatting of the sails and the faint sloosh of water against the hull. For a few moments he forgot about the race. He thought, instead, of the magic over there of Africa and the unreal gold of the evening sky above the Valley of the Kings in Egypt— places where time once before had deserted him, where he had been transported in years past to another age of primeval wonder.

Somebody was at his elbow. Aggressively, he turned.

Sally stepped backwards sharply. "I'll announce myself next time!" She looked at the fast-falling night and the blue beauty of it and then followed Nelson's pointing finger to the sinister form of the shark still discernible a few yards from the hull. Her voice changed to a whisper. "Even he looks lovely, doesn't he?" she hissed.

Nelson said nothing. He watched her silhouette as the rapidly falling darkness merged with her, his heart throbbing with lust for a second or two. "There's just you and me and a thousand miles," he said thickly, his voice barely more than a whisper.

She didn't reply.

Things were very different on board the Red Bird. The crew, galvanised by Steinhoff into a team imbued with Germanic efficiency, were not only determined to win but they were sure of their eventual victory. The navigator was bent over the chart now, plotting a coastal course down this part of Africa. Madeira and the Canaries were now behind them. The fleet was scattered, with *Der Rote Vogel* in the lead and the Hood in sight not far behind. The Americans and Russians were about 40 miles behind. The French were further out about 250 miles away. Turkey, Israel and Brazil were well out, south of the latitude of the Canaries. The Saudis and the Canadians were having a private race. West Germany was further to the west.

Steinhoff rubbed his hands as he looked at the chart, surveying the world as if he was a giant god contemplating his own creation. "We shall sail well inside the Cape Verde Islands," he told Bauer. "As close to the coast as we can."

Bauer, a square-chinned man with the blond hair and blue eyes of a handsome Nordic, disregarded Steinhoff's tactical discussion. "What did you make of it?" he asked his skipper.

Steinhoff looked up. "Make of what?"

"The bottle-screw."

Steinhoff smiled a shallow, evil smile which held only ruthlessness. "I am not now surprised." He handed Bauer a sheet of paper bearing a radio message which had come through earlier.

Bauer read it, stunned. "What will you do?"

There was a deep laugh from Steinhoff. "Do? I shall do nothing! Except keep a close check on the boat. We need the extra man to keep up a full complement. So that we can win! The politicians and the police can sort out their own problems when we are back home. All I want to do is to win."

Bauer was grim. "I cannot agree with you, Herr Kapitän. This man offers a threat to our country. We are, foremost, soldiers and sailors working for our country. That is our paramount duty."

There was a sigh from the other man. "So, what do you want me to do? Put into port? I am not going to do that. This man cannot go anywhere. He is locked on board this ship by the mighty ocean. He cannot get away from us. And while the sea traps him on board he can work for us and for his food."

"Where is he now?" asked Bauer.

"In his bunk, sleeping." Steinhoff was no longer concentrating on Bauer. Blenken was leaning through the hatchway with anxiety creasing his face. "What is it?"

"The British are catching up. They are only a couple of miles behind us now. And we cannot do much about it, because the wind has virtually all gone. Died on us. The Hood has held a little breeze of her own back there."

Steinhoff leapt up to the cockpit to see for himself and

then looked at what seemed like acres of drooping canvas hanging limply from the mast of his sloop. "Blast! Blast! Blast!" As he cursed he raised his eyes to the horizon, way over the port side. He could just make out a minutely slim pencil-sliver of misty blue merging with the sea on the brink of his vision. Africa.

Blenken nudged him with a smile. "The Hood is now becalmed, too. She has lost the wind."

"Good."

On the British yacht Nelson was surveying his own limp sails. He drifted his own curses across the lifeless sea.

"I thought we were going to have her," he murmured glumly. He turned to Good. "But it's not just the Germans that concern me."

Good swept his glasses round from *Der Rote Vogel* to the line of Africa on the horizon. "So what's bugging you, then?"

"Look right over there. Behind."

Good followed his pointing finger to two very small faint smudges right on the horizon over the stern of the Hood. "The Yanks and the Russians?"

"Must be. They must be catching us."

They watched mesmerised as the minutes grew into an hour. Then two hours. Then three. By now the two smudges of distant white were discernible as yachts, flying coloured spinnakers and white mainsails. It was late afternoon.

"They'll be past us during the night at that rate," said Good quietly.

Nelson shook his head. "I doubt it. We were hustling

along, remember? But then we hit the flat spot just like the Red Bird. They'll hit it, too."

But glumly they watched the two yachts grow closer behind and the night fall fast over the limp, dead sea. *Der Rote Vogel* was motionless, about half a mile in front. Behind were the Eagle and Vladimir. Quiet and still.

One recurring sound, however, etched its way remorselessly into the peace of the night . . . the voice of Pete Campbell. "This is British yacht Hood in Worldsail. I am testing damaged radio. If you hear me, please reply." The plea drifted answerless in the ether. Eventually he gave up and fell asleep.

Campbell awoke with a start in the grey of dawn, feverishly adjusting the set and waking Nelson by the movement. "I've got something," he whispered urgently.

"Good. I knew you'd do it in the end," muttered Nelson through the red mist of waking.

"Wait! It's only faint." He twiddled a few knobs. "Listen to that."

Nelson slipped on the headset. The words were faint . . . and in German. "Big bear to red bird. Big bear to red bird. Come in, please. Come in, please. Big bear to red bird . . ."

The two men glanced at each other. Nelson listened for several minutes and then started scribbling . . . "No change. Owl is still sleeping. Red bird still ahead. Hood behind. Eagle and Vladimir only several miles away. Over . . ."

. . . "This is bear. Hold owl. Repeat, hold owl. Prepare for submarine rendezvous 2300 hours tomorrow . . ."

Campbell shuffled uneasily. "It must be. It must be

them. Can't be anyone else, can it?" He stared at Nelson for confirmation.

Nelson was puzzled. "I don't like the smell of it. But if they break any race rules we've got 'em!" He paused, rubbing his eyes. "Better get some sleep."

The dawn rose on the four boats, their positions unchanged. It was hot and lazy. A small whale swam up to look at them curiously and then drifted away without interest, submerging for minutes at a time until it finally disappeared.

In the late morning, as three of the Hood's crew replaced the plywood patch in the bow with a permanent repair of glass fibre, Tooke had something better to photograph. Sally appeared *au naturel*, completely nude, to lap up the heat of the sunshine. Tooke quickly pointed his camera. Nelson looked her way open-mouthed. She knew she was being watched by the two men and she knew that she was beautiful, revelling in their attention, taunting them with her body, which gleamed in the tropical sun as she moved like liquid to the coach-roof, there to subside with a smile onto a big blue towel.

Nelson felt the stiffening in his loins and weakly whistled. "I'm sorry," he whispered in sorrow to Tooke, "but somebody's got to do it." He began to move forward.

"Do what?" asked Tooke, holding him back by the arm. "Keep your filthy hands off. She's the property of us all."

Nelson smiled. "That's what I'm worried about. It's like showing a single glass of whisky to a bunch of alcoholics who haven't had a drink for a fortnight!"

He marched up to Sally and stood above her. She lay on

her back, defiantly unmoving, her hands drawn up behind her head and her knees lifted. Smiling, she knew he was drinking in her body . . . breasts, legs, thighs, hair, the smoothness of her shoulders and her hips. And she stared up at him without moving, eye to eye, feeling the electricity she was generating in him.

Nelson swallowed hard. The words came out with a strange gruffness, as if they had had a struggle to get beyond the throat. "Sally . . . er . . . well . . ."

"Well what?" She stopped smiling with her mouth, but grinned with her eyes.

"Christ, get some bloody clothes on! You'll drive us all bloody crazy!"

She chortled and still did not move. But even as he ogled once more over those beautiful curves and the firm flesh of her breasts, her mood suddenly changed and she leapt up, drawing the towel over the front of her body. "All right," she snapped and angrily made her way back to the cockpit and down the hatchway, displaying a naked rear which left them as breathless as before.

Within seconds she reappeared in a scanty white bikini. Nelson shrugged and caught his breath. He turned to look at the competitors locked with the Hood as if someone up there was playing a gigantic game with them on the ocean.

Campbell appeared briefly in the hatchway and beckoned Nelson below.

"Confirmation about the rendezvous with the sub at 2300," he said.

Nelson nodded and made his way out again and along the deck to the bow, where work was just finishing. "Should hold out pretty well," said Le Strange, wiping the sweat from his face. "It's better than new, except for being a bit rough on the outside. We'll have to leave the wood backing. It'll give it strength."

Nelson smiled his satisfaction.

It was in the evening when Nelson, sitting alone at the bow, legs dangling over the side, heard it. A skirl in the water. Something was nearby. He could hear the faint, gentle gurgle of water pass the bow of the ghosting yacht. A shark? Or a whale? He felt the hair rise on his neck. God, if it was a whale they'd better look out smartly! He remembered the reports that he'd read from the survivors of yachts which had been holed and sunk by whales over the years. Mainly they had been killer whales—black whales with white viper vees on their necks, whales which hunted in packs and which launched attacks on boats, perhaps mistaking them for prey. He listened again. It was closer now. Certainly not an attack. It was too slow. He listened for the blow of the whale, but heard nothing except the faint sound of water being disturbed. He peered into the blackness, but there was nothing. Then he saw it. A liferaft. Containing one man. "Who the hell are you?" Nelson called out quietly.

"Don't ask me any questions," said the man breathlessly. "Just get me aboard quickly, will you?"

Nelson coiled up a rope. "Are you from *Der Rote Vogel*?" he called into the night, hoping his voice would not carry too far in the still air.

"Yes."

"So you're the Owl, then?"

"What's that?"

"Nothing. Grab this rope." He threw the coil down into the liferaft. It was taken immediately by the man, who burst the raft with a quick thrust from his knife as he climbed on board, holding out his hand towards Nelson.

"My name's Keller. I'm one of you." He smiled as they shook hands. "It's a matter of British security. I was going to paddle for the coast, but I lost my nerve as soon as I got into the raft. I can't swim. But it's important I remain safe."

Nelson surveyed him with suspicion. "Keep your voice down. You'd better explain what this is all about, otherwise you can go back down there where you came from."

Keller smiled confidently. "I told you. I can't swim. And the raft's sunk now."

Nelson replied sternly: "You can still go back if you don't put me in the picture . . . and drown for all I care."

Keller shrugged. He did not explain much, but enough to satisfy Nelson.

"Why didn't you stay on board *Der Rote Vogel*?"

"Because they know. I heard the radio."

"Is it you the submarine is after?"

"Yes."

"So you are the Owl, then?"

"Yes."

Nelson hissed at the man in a menacing whisper. "Just remember—I want to win this bloody race. And even you, Mister Owl, are not going to make any difference to that."

Keller, his long, pale face cracking into a beam, smiled in triumph. "Then there's no problem. I'm an extra hand. I can help you until you can put me ashore somewhere."

Keller's sudden appearance, out of the black of the night, evoked a few open mouths. After all, the chances of acquiring, without warning, a strange face during a round-the-world yacht race in the South Atlantic off the coast of Africa must be pretty remote. But Keller explained as he had explained to Nelson. Uneasily, reluctantly, the crew accepted him on board.

Campbell stared out from his earphones. "It is clear," he announced quietly, "that we are not the only people who have been eavesdropping on the Red Bird. Both the Americans and the Russians have heard, too. They have both been talking to their people on land."

Keller was not embarrassed to be the centre of interest. "Of course they know," he said. "It was a Russian sub that is supposed to take me off *Der Rote Vogel*. The Russians have good reason to prevent me reaching Britain." He chuckled to himself. "The Americans won't want me to, either."

Good looked at him, puzzled. "What do you mean?"

"Sorry," said Keller. "That I can't tell you."

Sally turned towards him. "Then tell me this. Are you English? Or German? Or what? You speak without an accent."

Keller merely smiled.

THREE

The dawn watch saw the sun rise like a smile on a gathering breeze which went some way to quell a new gloom on the Hood. At the helm was Campbell. Nelson and Sally were in the cockpit, warming themselves at the sight of *Der Rote Vogel* being overhauled. She was off the port bow about three hundred yards away, wallowing as the British boat inexorably made her way past into the open water which pointed the way south towards the Cape of Good Hope.

Keller was in the cockpit now. Nelson had his binoculars trained on the Red Bird. "Looks like they're having difficulty," he said.

"I wouldn't mind betting that the rudder is damaged," replied Keller, standing at his elbow. There was a twinkle in his eye.

Nelson, expecting Campbell and Sally to be the only other occupants of the cockpit, was startled at the sound of Keller's voice. "Hell, are you a fool?" he spat at Keller. "I don't want you seen . . . by the East Germans, by the Russians or by the Americans. I'd have thought that would have been clear enough to you, too."

Keller glanced back at the pursuing craft, both with huge

billows of canvas set as they raced like chariot horses just a couple of hundred yards apart and only about half a mile behind the Hood. He ducked down the hatchway without saying another word.

"Was he seen?" asked Campbell.

Nelson was looking at the Russians. "They're looking. I think both the Russians and the Americans are looking. Don't know about the Germans. Damn the man." He looked up at the sails on the Hood. They were full, canting the yacht over slightly as she converted the wind into forward power, easily slicing through the blue warm water with a shush-shush-shush and a wake of white. It was warm and the air was growing hotter with every minute that passed.

"Blow, wind, blow," muttered Nelson, peering over his shoulder. The Hood needed as big a lead as she could get before she hit the Doldrums. It was not merely a question of being ahead. Nelson now wanted the Hood to lose herself alone on the Atlantic, away from other eyes, away from trouble, away from the opposition.

Below, Le Strange pushed a plate of food under Nelson's nose. "Your breakfast, captain," he said with a wink. "And where's the lovely Lolita this morning?"

"In the cockpit," replied Nelson.

"Fully clothed or spouting hard little red nipples and naked crotch?"

"Jeans and tee-shirt, I'm afraid."

"Well, in that case you can have the pleasure of telling her that breakfast is ready."

Nelson shouted up at her and Campbell took over. Sally appeared hungrily.

"Where are the other boats now?" asked Nelson.

She smiled. "The Red Bird has fallen way behind. And we're pulling away from the other two."

They grinned. The gloom which had crept over them imperceptibly since Keller's arrival was lifting rapidly, like mist wafting away under the heat of the sun.

Quickly Nelson finished and returned to the cockpit. "Don't be long," he called to Sally as he went out into the warm air. "A watch is a watch. No concessions."

He went to take the helm from Campbell but Campbell was reluctant to hand over: "It's a beautiful sail and the Hood's a beauty. Look at that lead now." With satisfaction he nodded over his shoulder. The boats in pursuit were a couple of miles behind now. The East Germans were even further behind and with their sails down. "But I've been thinking. Won't we be disqualified for picking up an extra man?"

Nelson smiled. "No. The rules state that we are not allowed to take extra equipment on board but they also say that we can help anybody in distress. And I reckon that our Mr. Keller the Owl was in some distress, don't you?"

Campbell smiled, too. "I'll tune in if you like."

"All right, but tell Sally to get up here smartish. I shouldn't have to be on my own." It was to his own surprise that he heard himself say the words and then, to his further discomfort, found that he fidgeted until she was back in the cockpit with him, her return bringing a strange calm and completing what appeared to him at that moment to be something approaching perfection . . . the Hood in the lead, the sun baking down, a comfortable beam wind, huge area of sail aloft, every square inch filled with a live breeze, singing the yacht on her way, a sparkling wake . . .

"I hope this lasts," he said. Perhaps he meant more than it sounded.

She said nothing to him, either then or during the remaining two hours of the watch, during which time the Eagle and the Vladimir slipped further behind into the clear blue of distance and the Red Bird, now on her way again with sail billowing hard, behind those two and further inland.

For the rest of the day the Hood cleaved on, the wind picking up and adding even more power to the surge through the Atlantic, cheating the Doldrums out of a few miles of their artless guile.

That day and the next were the Hood's two best days of the race so far, putting just under 500 miles behind in those forty-eight hours, the yacht's log now warming to the race with glowing prose and optimism as each succeeding watch, with pen in hand, drank in the charge. The other three boats slipped out of sight below the pursuing horizon and by nightfall on that second day the driving Hood was at last alone again.

Inevitably it was Le Strange who suggested that the Hood should celebrate.

"A bit premature," said Nelson, but the rest of the crew ignored him. They wanted a party. Nelson protested. "We will only keep the lead if we keep our concentration, forcing every ounce of speed from the wind while we've got it." They took no notice.

Campbell came to him quietly as night darkened on that second idyllic day. "The other boats did see Keller. The radio is very faint but I'm picking up a few odds and ends.

The Russians, the Americans and the East Germans know that Keller is on this boat."

Nelson met the news with a shrug. "I suppose I suspected that all the time. Could you bring Keller to me? I think I'd better speak to him alone."

Keller came and they went to the foredeck, where the only sound was the bow slicing through the water. He faced Nelson without a word.

"Let's get it straight," said Nelson. "I'm willing to carry on round the world with you. But I'm equally happy to go on without you. It doesn't matter a damn to me. All that matters to me is carrying on in this race . . . and winning it. But if we're going to carry on with you on board I want to know a little bit more. Why should our friends the Americans, as well as the Russians, be embarrassed by your appearance in England?"

In the darkness, Keller's face was hardly visible. But Nelson knew it was not smiling. "I cannot tell you that. You must know that I am not at liberty to say anything."

Nelson was just as serious. "Normally, as it's a matter of security, I would not press you. But out here it's different. Little games like that between nations subside a little into triviality faced with the magnitude of the sea, of the sky, of the whole of nature. Can't you feel it? We rely on each other, a few simple people stripped to our fundamentals, to keep each other alive. One mistake by one person and we could all be dead. The sea is just waiting for that to happen. We lean on each other, and so we have to trust each other. Until you arrived on board we were fighting just the wind, the sea and any other elemental force that reared its ugly head in anger. Now there's more. There are three yachts not far behind, in radio contact with other people who know that you are on the Hood. There's a Russian submarine somewhere beneath us which probably knows as well. God knows who else does. And we can't contact anybody for help unless we put into port . . . and lose the race at the same time. It would make it just a wee bit easier to stomach if we knew precisely what we're up against—and why." He turned towards Keller. "Don't forget. The only people who appear to know that you are with us are people who want to get rid of you. They would probably help us to feed you to the sharks. If you don't co-operate with us here on the Hood we can get rid of you as easily as we like and nobody would care."

There was silence from Keller. Nelson was menacing. "Don't think that it's beyond us, just because we're British. We're in this for the race. We don't want to lose. Every day that passes means an extra day's allegiance to winning and a day's less allegiance to the head of Security. Don't even think that we wouldn't hand you over to the Americans—or the Russians—if it meant we could carry on. Just think about it for a minute."

"I don't have to," said Keller quietly. "I will tell you, because I understand." He breathed in deeply. "I have a list of probably the most explosive people in the world. I have a notation of what they do that makes them the most explosive people in the world. The British government, who employ me, have asked for it and that is my sole aim. I have the names of the most important Russian spies in Washington, London, France, West Germany and West Berlin. I have the name of the link—the person that the world's Press call 'The Courier'—between Moscow and most of the terrorist organisations of the world. But I also have the names of the CIA agents operating in both eastern and western Europe, including London and Paris, and what their operations are. That will open a few eyes in both Europe and the USA. I have information about the continuing leaks from NATO, information which would blow wide open the political situation in West Germany. And I have information which would cause great embarrassment to a certain group of loosely linked British members of Parliament."

"Led by?" Nelson was serious.

"Do I have to tell you?"

"Yes."

Keller hesitated. Then shrugged. "John Crane."

Nelson whistled. "You're right. That would blow it wide open." There was silence for a few moments. "Okay. Even though you're most people's eggs all in one basket, welcome aboard, Mr. Keller. Or do we call you Owl?"

"Just call me Keller."

Keller went aft and down into the cabin. Nelson stayed on the foredeck listening to the sweet music of the water against the hull, feeling the wind on his face and in his hair, hearing the odd strain from the rigging as the Hood ploughed on. He was more determined to win than he had ever been, determined to get to Britain before any other boat, to win and now, at the same time, to deliver up safely Keller and his cargo of words.

For the rest of that night the Hood agreed. The breeze strengthened until she was racing with her lee rail occasionally pressed under a wave, the spray tossing itself into the cockpit at times to catch the helmsman unawares.

Although the wind lightened again during the next day on went the Hood towards the South Atlantic, towards the home of the albatross, towards the world of relentless winds and waves, rogue waves, of cold and icebergs, of loneliness and the universe itself . . .

In the afternoon there was excitement on board the Hood. Campbell picked up a broadcast from Living Doll giving the positions of the racing yachts to the Brazilian boat. The Hood appeared to be well in the lead, possibly thirty-five miles ahead of the leading group and hundreds of miles ahead of the laggards.

The wind had dropped during the morning and had moved ahead towards the bow, so that the Hood was bubbling along against it through the heaving sea at eight or nine knots. The generator was recharging the batteries. Nelson was ebullient. His noon sight had given him a good fix and things seemed to be working out to plan. Tooke was pleased, too. One of the Atlantic's most lovable birds, the woolly-looking little Mother Carey's Chicken, had been huddled all morning on the lee deck out of the wind, providing him with some good shots of the bird with Sally, who had let her bikini drop for the occasion. Good was plotting a position near the thin eastern end of the Doldrums.

"We should be out of the north-east trades soon," Good told Nelson, as if they were about to say goodbye to an old friend. "We're now well past the Cape Verdes."

The Hood suddenly became quiet again as Nelson switched off the diesel generator, giving up the yacht to the hush of the sea against the hull and the occasional flap of canvas or rope.

It was a time of preparation. Tanner oiled moving parts of blocks, ratchets and slides during the morning. Howard examined mast fittings and rigging. There were still more than 3,500 miles to go before the lower tip of Africa and then more than 6,000 miles through the Roaring Forties to Australia. It was a long way off. But the power of those southern seas, many miles distant, began to loom in their hearts already while the hot sun climbed high into the blue sky as the Hood sailed on towards the equator. They were determined not to fail because of weakness whatever else might befall them in the wild loneliness that was yet to come.

Nelson peered behind, sweeping his binoculars backwards and forwards over the horizon. Tooke was at the helm.

"See anything?" asked Tooke, still with the Nikon slung round his neck.

"No." Nelson had a frown. "I thought I did a couple of hours ago but I must have been mistaken."

"Those other boats couldn't be catching us the way we've been going," said Tooke, his face raised, satisfied, towards the full white sails.

"I wasn't thinking about the Red Bird, or the Eagle or any of the others. I was thinking of a submarine. They're probably searching for us."

Keller, climbing out of the hatchway, heard. "We are too small to show on their radar. We have no engines to register noise or heat. We have every chance in the world of remaining undetected."

Nelson could not disagree but he was still anxious. "You must know as well as I do that submarines these days have very, very sophisticated methods of detection on board. And there are satellites which can pick out a flower pot on photographic film from up there in space. We're a bit bigger than a flower pot."

"Yeah, sure," replied Keller, unconcerned. "But we are in the great wide wastes of the Atlantic Ocean. It must be a billion to one against."

Nelson scanned the sea again. "I hope you're right."

There were shouts of joy from below, followed by the arrival on deck of Le Strange and Sally with a stained carton of rotten eggs. Le Strange cast them over the side and watched them disappear into the sea. "It's a pity about the lost protein, but I have another way of obtaining that."

"How?"

"My crossbow. If you see a turtle just shout. And if you find flying fish on board don't chuck them back just because they're small. Collect them and we'll fry them. They're supposed to be tasty. I might even try shark meat if you see one."

"Rather you than me." Sally shuddered.

"Come on, you old kill-joy," said Le Strange, poking Nelson in the arm. "Smile. Smile like you're happy, like we're winning, like the sun's shining. We're having our party after the sun's gone down and you can damn well enjoy yourself, even if we have to force you."

"You'll have to bring me a drink up here," said Nelson. "It's my trick at the helm. Besides, I want to keep my eyes open. It's too bloody quiet."

The quiet, for what it was, evaporated when darkness fell. The wind had dropped a little further to make sailing the Hood a comfortable occupation. All was at peace. But for the crew it was going to be a night of merriment, a pagan feast to celebrate nothing and anything . . .

They began drinking in the early evening, all except Nelson, who was soberly stroking the helm to keep the Hood driving on southwards. Within two hours he was the only really sober person on board. Le Strange was leading the singing. The others joined in a mammoth chorus which rang across the water, the sound spinning out over the sea, an incongruous intrusion into nature's brief sleep of darkness under a sultry blanket of warmth which did not subside with the passing of the sun into its black velvet bed.

Le Strange threw back the contents of his glass and tried to focus on the table. He poured another drink. The rest now, except Sally, were beyond the stage of total merriment, drinking quietly, almost soberly. It was as if the alcohol had brought home to them the enormity of what they were undertaking, leaving them only the empty satisfaction of contemplation where once there had been optimism.

Throwing his arms clumsily around Sally's neck, Le Strange leant towards her. He raised his glass. "To the female members of our crew," he chortled drunkenly.

She giggled. "You've toasted me already." She bathed in the warm glow of the drink. "I'm glad we decided to have this little party."

Le Strange leant closer. "You're drunk."

"Yes," she chuckled, gulping at her glass but managing to collect only part of the drink swilling around her lips. The rest trickled down her chin and onto the clean flesh above her bikini top. She laughed loudly and squirmed as Le Strange wiped his forefinger down her chin and followed the line of liquid down her neck. "Off, off! Bob Le Strange, you're a lecher."

He swigged his glass and held it up. "And here's to lechery," he said. "Come on. Let's go up on deck and see what old Tom is up to."

"Right." She jumped up to her feet, immediately finding that she had to hang on. "Whoops! Tom bloody Nelson! Keep this boat level, will you?" Her voice was slurred but happy. Le Strange went up on deck.

Nelson stood quietly at the wheel, his eyes looking ahead but not seeing in his peaceful solitude.

"Enjoying yourself?" inquired Le Strange, rolling over to him and leaning on his shoulder. "Follow the dog star, old chap! That way lies a treasure store of wicked women and hard liquor awaiting lost sailors and ship-wrecked me-hearties."

Nelson leant away from Le Strange's heavy breath. He refused to have his reverie interrupted and so did not join in. He stared distantly into the blackness and merely said, "Mmmmm."

Le Strange's staggering departure towards the foredeck coincided with the appearance of Sally, tee-shirted now above her bikini in the warmth of the night. She waved, giggly and happily, to Nelson. She had a glass in her hand, the other hand grabbing a guard rail to prevent her losing balance. Slowly, deliberately, she made her perilous way forward. Nelson silently watched her go.

She found Le Strange leaning over the pulpit, gazing down at the bow wave. She staggered towards the rail and held on tightly, her glass spinning into the sea, her eyes shut against the whirling of the world. Le Strange moved over and pulled her away from the edge of the boat, muttering something about safety. She felt drunkenly detached from herself, unable to move, as he roughly held her cheeks between the thumb and fingers of one hand and pushed his lips against hers, the sweet taste of drink cloying around their mouths. She grunted in vain protest as his other hand surged into her tee-shirt and into her bikini top, massaging her breasts in deep movements while she weakly pushed against his forearms in an attempt to free herself. He released neither his hands from her breasts nor his face from hers. She struggled for breath and for something to hold onto, dizzy in mind and feeling. He staggered against her and they fell together onto the hard deck, Le Strange tearing at her bikini with a firmness which she knew she had no power to resist.

Within a moment he was deep inside her, thrusting, thrusting, surging breathlessly into her body, his weight pressing down on her chest, knocking the wind from her. "Please don't! No . . ." She protested as she caught her breath and pulled her mouth away from his, but he stifled her low cries with another rough kiss despite the anxious movement of her head from side to side as she fought to gain breath and, vainly, to push him off. Oh God, no! She felt his orgasm rising in great, massive pulses and clutched for breath as her own welled up in shame from deep within her loins to meet the last urgent lunging thrusts of his grunting climax.

He was spent.

She turned away, tears of frustrated anger rolling silently into the wisps of hair scattered around the flushed side of her face.

Le Strange rolled off and pulled himself to his feet, zipping himself up, his body still quivering and heaving for breath. He grinned down at her with a thick leer.

As he moved away aft she rolled over, burying her face into the stark hardness of the deck. "God, no. No. No. No!" Unable to quell the desperation of her physical weakness, of her lack of strength to keep him at bay, she sobbed for a second, frustrated in her blurred inebriation at having been able to do nothing about it. Her face ached. Breathing deeply to regain control she sat up and pulled on the scrap of bikini lying wrinkled, flimsy and small on the deck.

For several minutes she was motionless, listening to the surge of a different world, of water against the bow, of hushed undulating power of the Hood embraced by the kiss of the sea. She rose and pulled herself aft to the cockpit, where she sat in silence on the slatted teak of the seat. She looked at Nelson. He stared forward, distant and unspeaking. Had he seen? What did he think? Should she complain to him?

She said nothing. She remained there until early in the morning, when Nelson handed over the helm and silently moved below.

"I'll make you some coffee," she said.

She felt empty and dead.

As she brought his coffee their eyes met for a quiet flicker of time. She went to her berth and lowered herself into an uneasy doze, a shallow restless sleep of sadness and fury which mingled with the heavy snoring and grunting dreams spread through the other bunks.

When Nelson awoke the Hood was all bustle and movement. Last night's mess had been cleared away and breakfast eaten. But there was a heavy underlay of quietness, a tense silence radiating around Le Strange, his big, bearded frame erect and unrepentant in the galley.

"What's up?" Nelson glanced inquiringly from face to face.

"Ask him." Campbell jerked his thumb over his shoulder at Le Strange.

Nelson looked briefly in that direction. "Come on. We've got work to do. Is the radio fixed yet?"

Campbell shook his head. "We can't transmit. Some things we appear to be able to pick up. It's all too intermittent—merely a few seconds at a time if we're lucky. And so faint sometimes you might just as well not be hearing anything at all."

"Any chance of putting it right?"

"Doesn't look like it."

Nelson grimaced. "Have you picked up anything from the fleet?"

"No."

Nelson went up on deck, where Tanner was at the helm. "Seen anything?" asked Nelson.

"Two dolphins, a sperm whale and a biggie shark," replied Tanner. "We also collected five flying fish which will be on our breakfast plates tomorrow. There's also the bird."

He pointed to an albatross wheeling high above the Hood, its massive wings gliding effortlessly through the air above the long, low smoothing humps of sea.

"Must be pretty rare to see one this far north," muttered Nelson. "Hope it's a good omen."

"I shouldn't count on it." The sudden interruption came

from Keller. He spoke in low tones. "I'm sure I heard engines during the night. If they're searching for us there could be trouble."

The sea was empty. "Are you sure?" asked Nelson. "Nobody was in a fit state last night."

"Okay, I know. There might have been nothing there at all. I was a bit stewed." The sun beat down mercilessly as he spoke. He screwed his eyes and looked up at the limp sails. "Does that mean we have hit the Doldrums?"

"Yes."

"How are we going to play them?" asked Good. "What are our tactics? Are we going to chase every catspaw we see or do we sit tight and use every wind as and when it comes?"

"We sit tight," answered Nelson. "We can chase the breeze until we end up right up our own arseholes . . . but we won't. We'll concentrate on using every single ounce of wind that flows over us. We'll tack like a dinghy if necessary."

They were joined by Sally, wearing blue sweater and jeans.

"A little overdressed, aren't we?" Nelson's comment was ignored.

"Are we back on the air again?" Her smooth skin shone in the sunlight.

"No."

She pursed her lips, puzzled. "That's funny, then."

"What is?"

Sally shrugged. "Oh, it's probably nothing. We all had too much to drink last night."

"You speak for yourself," muttered Nelson. "Anyway,

you were saying . . . What do you think is funny?"

"It's probably nothing. I was sure I heard a radio transmitting morse during the night."

"Transmitting? You couldn't have. The transmitter's dead," said Nelson with scorn. "You were boozed up." But he thought for a moment about what Keller had said. "Well, perhaps it's not impossible. If there was a sub close we could have heard engine noise on the air and radio noise through the water. We'll just have to keep our ears and eyes skinned." Keller disappeared below.

Seeing him go, Tanner spoke up. "We just want to get on with the damn race. If anybody wants trouble surely we can just hand Keller over. He's big enough to look after himself. He knew what risks he was taking—it's all part of his job. But it's not our job. I don't see why we should start taking risks just for him and, frankly, I don't see why we should get involved at all, particularly if it's the Americans who want him and not the Russians. The Yanks are on our side, after all."

Tooke fiddled with his camera. "I can't agree. Tom, if you want to keep them away from Keller, I vote we fight all the way."

"Piss off," said Tanner, but without venom.

"I want to win this race as much as you," continued Tooke. "But I don't think Keller's going to make any difference—except to provide another couple of hands."

Nelson held up his hands. "All right. All right. Don't let's fight over it. For the moment we don't intend to let his presence on board make any difference."

Good and Howard joined them grimly. "I'm with you, Tom," said Howard.

"For Christ's sake, Geoff," said Good angrily, "if there's any trouble—and certainly if we're approached by the Yanks, I say we hand Keller over. We don't owe him anything."

A voice boomed over from the hatchway. Keller's long face beamed out across the cockpit. "Don't I get a say? I'm with you, Tom."

Another voice filtered up from behind Keller. "Me too." It was Le Strange.

"Looks like we carry on the good fight," said Nelson. "Now let's see what the wind's doing."

They looked round at the sails, which were drooping limply in the still air. The long flat roll of the sea rattled the boom from side to side.

The Hood had arrived in the Doldrums.

FOUR

They sat there, motionless save for the rolling of the sea, for the next two days under the searing sun which scorched down without mercy from a blue sky sullied only in two small fudgey places by the fluff of clouds moving across its unforgiving face. The crew of the British boat watched in frustration as squalls coming with the clouds ruffled the smooth surface of the sea a mile or two away. The Hood drifted, rolling slowly in her own patient frustration, murmuring occasional discontent through the slatting of the sails.

Sally broke the silence. "I heard it again last night."

"Heard what?"

"The transmitter."

"Why haven't we all heard it, then?" Le Strange spoke as he handed out bread and fruit. "That's the last of the apples for this week. I've decided to ration out the goodies."

Sally looked at him coldly.

He flicked her chin in a taunt and winked. "When do we have our next party?"

She pulled her head away and went to the opposite side of the cockpit. Le Strange went to follow her, grinning.

"Leave her alone," said Nelson sternly. "Just leave her alone."

Le Strange shrugged. "Must be the time of the month, I suppose."

Apart from the deck watch they went below early that afternoon, tired of the stillness of the air, tired of the heat of the sun, which showed no pity, tired of the uneasy creaking of the rigging and the rolling of the boom against the rope which held it.

"I tell you I did hear something," protested Sally.

"If you heard it we'd all hear it," said Tooke. "You're getting neurotic."

She stood up angrily. "No I'm not getting neurotic. I heard morse. As clear as I can hear you now. Morse. Do you know what that is? Diddidditdaditdadit. Ever heard of it?"

"Get stuffed," retorted Tooke.

"Yeah," leered Le Strange, smiling.

"Why can't you all accept what I say?" she asked pleadingly.

"Because," said Good, "you're getting your knickers in a twist. Or, at least, somebody's been twisting them for you."

She leapt up and slapped him hard across the face. Nelson grabbed her wrist. "Sit down! We've got enough problems without you getting histrionics."

She walked haughtily out of the saloon and up onto deck in a huff.

Campbell looked over at Le Strange. "You're a bastard, Bob. What you did was not screwing. It was more like bloody rape—and you're proud of it."

Good, Tooke and Nelson tensely watched the two, who glared at each other. Le Strange was the first to turn away. He went into the galley and busied himself with the evening meal.

Nelson turned to Campbell. "Give it a rest. Perhaps she enjoyed it."

Campbell rounded on him. "You were up there. Why the hell didn't you stop it? Couldn't you see that she was drunk and that he was going to stuff the arse off her any way he could?"

Sadly Nelson turned away. After a second or two he sighed. "I didn't think it was any of my business. Anyway, I didn't see what you say took place. Neither did you. You and all the rest . . . you're just speculating."

Campbell snorted angrily. "That bastard doesn't deny it, does he?"

Silence descended upon the Hood—the kind of silence that only the Doldrums can bring, a quiet punctuated by the sound of moving without getting anywhere.

Darkness fell, twilight finding Nelson arriving on the foredeck, where Sally was leaning on the pulpit rail. She didn't look up, but she spoke. "Keep away from me. I don't want you near me."

"You've heard what the others are saying?"

"Yes." Her voice betrayed nothing.

"Is it true?"

She glanced up. "Go and ask him! You're all men together, aren't you?" She grabbed his hand and thrust it onto her breast. "Go ahead! Have a good feel. That's what you all want, isn't it? You're all pigs at heart." He drew his hand away as she continued bitterly. "It doesn't matter anyway. I can look after myself. I only do what I want to do. I don't want your help. And I don't need it."

Nelson was equally stern. "Don't think I want to help you. You get all you ask for. No, what I'm concerned about is the Hood and the crew. A happy ship is more likely to be a winning ship in this race than an unhappy one . . . and I want the Hood to be happy. At the moment it is not. And you're one of the reasons."

She huffed noisily. "Of all the bloody cheek and nonsense! That's typically bloody male, isn't it? Blame the woman every time. Don't raise a word against the sacred phallus!"

He was embarrassed. "I wasn't talking just about that," he said levelly. "I was talking about the morse."

"You can believe it or not as you wish. I don't care. I know what I heard and I can't help that or alter it. Does it threaten you, little man?" She stared at him with anger.

He made no reply but went back to the cockpit and Good. "What if she did hear something?"

"Have you asked Campbell?"

"Yes. He says it wasn't him. We can't transmit. In any case, we've got nothing to transmit."

Good shrugged. "I don't really see what all the fuss is about. Sparky Campbell's been fiddling about with that damn radio every spare minute. He has picked up voices every now and again. He's also picked up morse amongst the dross."

Nelson shook his head. "At the time of night that she's heard it?" They stiffened suddenly as the sound of splashing carried through the air. They listened.

Nothing.

For several more minutes they strained their ears for a sound. But nothing.

Keller emerged from the darkness of the deck forward of the hatch.

"I didn't see you come out," said Nelson, relieved to have the tension broken.

"You two were too engrossed in chat," said Keller.

"Did you hear that splashing?"

"Yeah, but it's probably just a fish or a shark or a whale or something. It's their sea, not ours."

Nelson sat back on the teak slats behind the wheel. "You're right, Keller. We're all getting a bit fraught. Let's cool it, shall we? We'll come through it better and quicker."

But that night he thought he heard it, too. He was lying awake in the top forward bunk opposite the bunk occupied by Sally. If she was awake she was not showing it. He listened again. For a moment there was nothing, and then he thought he heard it again, so faintly that it could have been coming from a mile or two away. He lowered himself out of the bunk, wearing only his pants, and slipped towards the cockpit, keeping his ears craned for noise. There was not a sound in the Hood except the breathing of the dead-asleep. He popped his head out of the hatch and whispered to Tooke at the helm. "Did you hear anything?"

"Like what?"

"Anything."

"Not a thing, except that boom on the guy."

"Anybody up there with you?"

"Nope. I sent them down for a kip."

Nelson went back to his berth. Again he looked over

towards Sally and shook his head. He could not blame Le Strange. But the thought gave him a sharp pang. And that troubled him.

There was no time to remember his thoughts next day. For dawn broke with a bang.

"All hands on deck!"

The order shook sleep from their brains as if they had been hit with a sledgehammer. The crew, including Nelson, scurried up onto the deck to meet the warmth of the day . . . and the appalling, dismaying sight behind. A couple of miles away, driving on in the teeth of a squall which had not yet arrived over the Hood, was the Vladimir, looking as sinister as the clouds which carried her, huge red 'chute billowing stiffly as she curled under the power of the wind surging her along. As if still joined by a stretched umbilical cord, the Eagle was not far behind.

"Sod it! They're all coming our way," muttered Nelson. Keller glanced back anxiously. Nelson noticed that he was tying his lifejacket. "Why are you doing that?"

"Just in case there's any thought of handing me over," said Keller seriously. "I'll take my chance with the sharks. Africa can't be that far away."

Nelson scanned the sea with his binoculars. "It's worse than you think," he said grimly.

"Can't be."

"It is." He slipped the glasses off his neck and handed them to Keller. "See for yourself. *Der Rote Vogel* is within sight, too. A long way off, but in sight."

"Shit." Keller perused the horizon in silence. He looked at the Vladimir. "Have you had a close look at the Reds?"

"No."

"There's something odd going on." He shuffled uneasily. The Russians were gaining fast and the wind had not yet hit the Hood. Behind the Vladimir the Eagle was approaching at the same speed.

Nelson looked, too. "I think they're preparing to board us," he said in amazement. He became urgent and agitated. "Blow, you bugger of a wind. Blow."

Anxiously they waited for the black squall to arrive. Then it hit them.

The Hood laid over for a second as the sails filled, then, once her inertia was overcome, she rose and surged forward, just as the Vladimir rode up, pushing back a crest of white on either side, within hailing distance. A megaphone voice bit through the vibrant air . . .

"You have the East German Hans Mann on board. We have a request from *Der Rote Vogel* for us to take him from you so that when they catch up we can hand him over."

Nelson cupped his hands and shouted against the wind. "We can hand him over ourselves to *Der Rote Vogel*." The howl of the wind over the stern of the boat drowned his words.

The megaphone voice came through the wind again. "We are coming alongside." Nelson could see that one of the three men on the Vladimir's foredeck had a grapple, which was going to be thrown over the Hood for the coupling.

"Piss off!" Nelson moved the helm and the Hood, at the summit of a big wave, surfed forward so fast that Howard was bowled over, grabbing the deck as he slipped to leeward but sliding on with nothing to hang on to. Campbell grabbed him and Nelson breathed again with relief. A man overboard now and Keller would have to swim for it!

It grew darker as they flew along in the teeth of the squall, the Vladimir about a hundred yards off the stern on the port quarter. The Eagle was catching up fast, but the Vladimir was gaining on the Hood again. Nelson felt the rudder harden against a surging wave passing beneath the Hood and kept her steady. She surfed forward, just as the pursuing boats made their own runs on the backs of the Atlantic waves and gained on the Russians once more, then falling back as the Vladimir, in her turn, accelerated on a new crest. The lighter American boat took advantage of the waves to ride right up on the Russians, so that now the Eagle and the Vladimir were neck and neck . . . about 75 yards behind, the dramatic pursuit heightened now by jagged lightning which seared the sky and the sea in quick stabs cleaving the roar of the wind, waves and thunder.

Nelson felt the electricity surging through him in the excitement. The Hood tore along, bucking through the dark sea like a wild horse suddenly given his head. On they surged, glancing behind, a fox on the run, hunted, running, breathless . . .

"Harden that port spinnaker sheet," ordered Nelson.

There was immediate disaster. A quick rending pierced the rush of the wind and sea like a scream and the spinnaker billowed out wildly, a kaleidoscope of frenzied colours blowing frantically before the Hood in a flurry of noise, flapping and spray, while the boat bucked more upright, freed from the press of the huge sail.

Dismayed, Nelson could see what was wrong. The sheet had pulled out of the sail, taking a square yard of nylon with it.

"Haul down the 'chute!" As the crew on the foredeck struggled to get it down, the other two yachts surged up on the stricken British boat.

"There's no time," said Good. "We'll have to hand him over."

"Get the 'chute!" screamed Nelson above the wind. "We've still got a chance."

But the Vladimir was nearly up to them, with a crewman swinging his grapple, ready to throw. He launched it, but it fell a few yards short. Nelson breathed again, catching the welcome crest of a new wave to send the Hood surging forward down the massive rolling face of curling water to take the yacht further ahead again. The Russians latched on to a wave of their own and up they came again, the crewman retrieving the line and grapple as far as he could. On, too, came the Eagle, level now with the Vladimir, ahead now, behind now, as the Vladimir sucked more power from the wind and sea. The Hood creamed on, the noise of crashing water vying with the wind to tear at their minds.

It was then that the halyard parted. There was a sharp crack as the rope shot into two. The crew of the Hood hung in a suspended dismay, floating through static time, while the big billowing sail surged forward, unleashed at its top, in a strange fluttering slow motion, a peace which shattered with an enormous tear as the spinnaker hit the water. The boat sailed right over it. For the Hood it was like hitting a brick wall. The sudden resistance pulled her up, away from any further chance of surfing down the impatient waves in the unabating frenzy of the squall, which now thrust in its spear even deeper, unleashing a storm of rain at them amid the chaos of the lightning and the crashing, solid water.

Nelson ducked as a whirl of rope passed overhead. The Russians were almost alongside and this was the grapple, swinging fast through the air, right over the cockpit and then being pulled back by the Russian crewman so that it held fast and tight to the aft rail on Nelson's right. He swung the helm over but the grapple held them fast by the stern. The Hood careered round, the taut rope from the grapple pressing firmly into Nelson's back, flinging him across the cockpit like a catapulted stone. Landing in a bundle, he reached out vainly in an attempt to crawl back, a searing pain in his skull blurring everything, reaching wildly into nothing, a blackness . . .

Keller flung himself at the Russian rope like a wolf at its prey. He tore with his knife at the thick, twisted nylon, fraying it twist by twist until . . . bang! It parted with a rifle-like shot, the grapple slipping overboard on one side and the rope curling out into the sea back towards the flying Vladimir. Good hauled himself aft to the wheel and the Hood charged on again under control. Nelson staggered back to him through the torrential rain bursting down upon them in their desperation.

If they had any thoughts about giving up, the Eagle changed their minds for them, squeezing up between the Hood and the Vladimir and hardening in her sails, burying her nose into the flying spume and then pulling up into the wind. The Eagle heeled hard over, leaving the skipper of the Vladimir with a poor choice. She could storm on into the hull of the Eagle, or she could give way, forced up into the wind by the Americans. Inches separated the two yachts as they bucked together with the violent waters, creaming forward like the Hood at around 12 knots.

The Vladimir admitted defeat. Rather than smash into the Eagle she hardened up herself, heeled over and gave way, driving up into the wind as both yachts sailed up close-hauled away from the Hood.

The battle moved away into the distant darkness, into a confusion of water and searing rain. Nelson offered a prayer for America. His crew was now hoisting the bright blue storm spinnaker on a new halyard . . . and once more the Hood gathered in her skirts, not daring to look behind.

They raced through the night, hoping that the other two yachts would be carried away from them out of sight. Heeled over, pressed down by the sails as far as they dared, the Hood rushed on into the thick darkness, the whole boat pervaded by noise and wet, oilskins and equipment thrown around by the violent motion.

By morning there was no trace of the squall. Or of the pursuing boats. They were alone again on the Atlantic, sweating under the clear, burning equatorial sun, a bright orb of such searing brightness that they had to screw their faces into tight sunburned knots.

The crew rested.

Throughout the next three days more squalls, but none as violent or as prolonged, overtook the Hood. Alert to the whims of the wind, Nelson pushed her through the Doldrums, hanging on to the shirt-tails of any breeze that brushed against their cheeks. But the progress through this fickle belt of frustration was only a flickering joy to Nelson's troubled mind.

Why had the Americans fended off the Vladimir? Was the mysterious transmitter noise real and, if so, was it coming from inside the Hood . . . and why, who and with what? Could it be Campbell? Was it Keller, the man with the greatest vested interest in communicating with the outside world? If it wasn't one of those two, who else could it be? Did somebody want to let the Russians or the East Germans know where the Hood was?

He made up his mind that the only way to keep morale from flagging was to get to the bottom of the mystery surrounding the morse transmission.

The Hood was now, in her southerly push, almost on the equator itself, virtually out of the grey area between the Doldrums and the monsoon winds spreading out from Africa, and into the more constant south-east trades. They should hit the trades right on the nose if they headed towards Cape Town at the foot of the continent. This was the problem over which Nelson and Good pondered. The position of the windless South Atlantic High varied from year to year and from month to month as it drifted around the southern end of the Atlantic from South America to Africa like a lazy tramp without a home. The Hood had to try to avoid it at all costs. But to head east of the southerly course would probably be too slow, for they would almost certainly have to punch straight into the south-east trades and big seas. To head south directly would take them more or less into the area where they estimated the High to be. To head slightly west of south would take them further out into the Atlantic, would probably keep them going faster despite the extra distance; and they should then pick up the constant westerlies as they turned to port, heading beneath the African Cape of Storms and across the great southern ocean in the Roaring Forties, where the huge winds swept round the world virtually unchecked on the latitude of forty degrees south and beyond in the shrieking fifties, where the seas, unrelenting, flowed around the globe in mountains, whipped by merciless gales. It was the Clipper Way, the romantic route of the old square-riggers, a world of gales and of the wheeling, gliding albatross, where there was no help . . .

Nelson chose the westerly route—west, at least, of the Ascension Isles and St. Helena—to give them the best possible advantage from the sweeping westerlies at the end of the southerly punch . . . and to take them as far away as possible from the Russians, the Americans and the East Germans.

That afternoon Campbell picked up a message from Cape Town to the fleet giving the positions of the racing yachts. The Americans, Russians and East Germans, still close to each other, were behind the Hood's own estimated position but closer to the African coast. Level on latitude, but way over on the other side of the Atlantic, far, far to the west were the French, about 400 miles ahead of West Germany. Between the two groups, in the central Atlantic, were the Saudis. About 250 miles behind them to the north-west came Canada and another 200 miles behind them came Israel. Brazil was more or less level on latitude but well into the African coast north of Monrovia, and Turkey was behind, within sight of the Cape Verde Islands. A long way behind were the Italians.

Nelson grunted, satisfied.

The equator was now behind the Hood. They drove on southwards, snatching whatever breeze they could, gathering rain when they could, drinking in the sun which they knew would gradually be left behind. If anybody heard again the mysterious phantom transmissions they were saying nothing; a lull in a quiet, efficient period during which the crew relished hard work on deck, occasionally spotting a dolphin or a school of porpoise, perhaps an albatross or some of the smaller silvery prions, birds which popped up from nowhere to swoop on scraps thrown over the stern.

They picked up the south-east trades, put on their oilskins and prepared for a hard slog to windward, with the wind coming over the port bow, heeling them over at thirty degrees as the Hood powered on. They slammed through the big, sweeping waves, throwing up spray and green water. Everything which the Hood met she shrugged aside.

And all the time Nelson watched and listened, while the others felt the tension amongst them subside in the communal effort to reach the Roaring Forties.

The peace came to an end as the sun rose on a spectacular dawn revealing St. Helena as a smudge to port. Sally was at the helm, her fine skin weathered to a nutty brown, adding sparkle to her long, blonde hair. Her eyes shone with the beauty of the sunrise and she was smiling. The Hood was romping along at the same angle which she had assumed for hundreds of miles now. They were adjusting to it. Tooke was sitting on the foredeck watching the dawn and taking photographs.

There it was again! She could hear it. For a few minutes

there came the morse. Then it stopped. She cast her eyes on a long sweep round the yacht, over the yellow rolling waves on one side and the dark indigo water on the other.

She called forward. "Did you hear that, John?"

"What?"

"The same old thing. That transmitter."

Tooke frowned. "No. Do you want me to call the skipper?"

"You'd better."

Tooke went below and shook Nelson in his bunk. "Skipper, come on, skipper. Wake up." But Nelson's eyes were already open.

"I heard it myself," said Nelson. "I also heard somebody around in the dark."

Another voice piped up from the stern, shafting through the boat's sea sounds. "That could have been me going to the heads." It was Keller.

Nelson raised an eyebrow. "Go and bring Keller here to me."

Tooke returned with Keller, who was still pulling on his white sweater.

"Did you hear the radio?" asked Nelson.

"No."

"Sit down." He motioned Keller to sit down next to him on the bunk. "There's nothing personal, you understand. I want you to sit there while John takes a look around your berth."

"What if I object?" Keller stared menacingly at Nelson.

"We'll look anyway." Nelson jerked his thumb in command at Tooke.

Tooke searched. "There's nothing."

Nelson's face creased into a smile. "Okay, that's all, Keller. You know we had to check."

Keller shrugged. "If you say so. It doesn't bother me." He went up on deck as if nothing had happened.

"What do you make of it?" asked Tooke.

Nelson had no answer for him. "It looks as if somebody is transmitting from this boat."

Tooke shook his head. "I don't honestly believe there's anything to it."

Nelson shrugged. "I hope you're right."

They were in the south-east trades, unmolested in a peace which returned as suddenly as it had been broken, for nearly 3,000 miles. Then they headed east, unable to make further radio contact with anybody, heading for the southern tip of Africa where, a hundred miles offshore, they would have to pass within sight of the South African marker ship.

The Hood, to the immense relief of the crew, missed the South Atlantic High and toasted her skipper by clapping her skirts around the strong westerlies for a sizzling, rolling spinnaker run towards the Cape of Good Hope . . . the Cape of Storms, a name of awe bestowed upon it for good reason by seamen down through the ages. Occasionally the wind dropped or turned its head like a fickle woman but the Hood shrugged it aside, rising to the massive waves which ran at her, threatening to overwhelm her if she should put a foot wrong.

The marker ship was spotted by Le Strange from the masthead. But he saw smething else, which brought him down in a scurry in the bosun's chair. "We are not alone," he muttered.

The others looked at him.

"Three sails. We're still ahead—but not by much."

The Hood sailed close to the South African vessel, Good signalling that the radio was out of action.

"Tell them we don't want any help," ordered Nelson. "We'll keep working at getting the radio going."

It was the only time of tension for some days, except for the two times they were buzzed by light aircraft from the direction of the Cape. But nothing happened and the three pursuing yachts remained hidden beneath the brow of the horizon. Forty days out of England now and they were alone again, the Roaring Forties finding their voice in the reefed-down sails, the Hood buffeting along on that long road east. But it was a time of foreboding rather than of happiness. They felt as if they were entering a huge vacuum of spiritual emptiness. And they felt alone. Nelson almost wished he could see the Russians or the East Germans for company, but even on the tops of the moving mountains of water which swept on in their vastness he could see nothing.

The shortest distance between Cape Town and New Zealand—roughly 7,500 miles depending on which crow's route you take—is not immediately apparent on a normal atlas map. It is more easily discernable on a three-dimensional globe, just as are the shortest air routes of the world. On a globe it is easy to see these Great Circle tracks which follow the curve of the earth between any two points. Following the shortest curve from the Cape of Good Hope to

New Zealand, the line passes right across the ice and snow-bound wastes of the solid continent of Antarctica. A yacht, therefore, has to modify that shortest line for its route, not merely to avoid the great hulk of that barren world standing in the way but to avoid its fringe of icebergs, which creep north in the frozen gale-swept winters and shrink back south again during the Antarctic summer. The choice also has to take into consideration the continuation of that ice limit beyond New Zealand for another 6,000 miles to the notorious Cape Horn.

It was not an easy decision for Nelson to make, to order his boat either north—adding greater distance in those vast lonely wastes of ocean—or south, adding the risk of iceberg collision to all the other hazards which confronted them. The thrill of changing charts from the Atlantic Ocean to the Indian Ocean soon evaporated as the chill of the Roaring Forties and the desolation of those southern seas struck deeply home.

Good scratched his head. "If we play it by the book and keep to the advice of The Ocean Passages of The World we ought to stick to latitude forty degrees or not much further south. But . . ."

Nelson was not listening. He thought of the massive seas in the notorious waters over the Agulhas Bank off Africa.

He breathed in deeply. "We go south!"

FIVE

"I don't believe it." Campbell, hunched over his radio, listened intently.

Nelson rose from the saloon table, braced himself against the slamming of the boat and lurched over to Campbell, holding on to the grab rail in the cabin. "What have you heard?"

Campbell raised his hand for quiet. "What's our position?"

"Fifty-six south . . . about fifty east," replied Good.

Campbell looked up in horror. "That's the position which has just been given for us on the radio. They've got our position."

"Who are 'they'?"

Campbell shrugged. "Who knows? Somebody talking to the Eagle. They're behind us."

Le Strange lurched from the galley. His face was black. "Why don't you stop playing with that bloody thing? It gives me the shits. Even with gales and that sea out there the only time I worry is when you're on the radio."

"Calm down," snapped Nelson. "You—"

"Piss off!" retorted Le Strange. "I'd rather not know,

that's all." He pointed at Keller. "He's the bloody cause of it. Let's pitch him over the side."

Keller looked up, smiling. But it was a cold smile.

The yacht lurched into a wave trough, flinging Le Strange against the galley side. Nelson pulled himself across the galley door. "Cool it, Bob. We've got enough to contend with without you getting paranoid."

"Paranoid!" Le Strange spat the word out. "Paranoid? How can you expect us not to get paranoid with him on board with his little fucking mysteries and half the fleet trying to get up our arse?"

But they were now in the Roaring Forties, where the constant battle against the elements meant that Nelson could split the crew roughly into two, one half working on deck trimming sails or helming, the other half resting or asleep below. The joker in the pack, Le Strange, was required to stay in the galley most of the time.

The strain mounted. The constant banging of the Hood in the big swirling seas meant a continuing personal battle for each one of them against the slamming yacht herself. One slip below decks could mean serious injury. A slip on deck could be worse. There would probably be little hope for anybody who went overboard, either slipping over or being washed over. They wore their red oilskins and life-lines. Howard struggled to keep the Hood on course. Good, hanging onto the starboard shrouds, was keeping an iceberg watch. Nelson, clipped into the cockpit, was watching behind.

That afternoon it snowed.

But they had no time to wallow in their cold misery.

"Behind us!" called Nelson urgently. "They've caught

us."

"How far?" asked Howard in resigned gloom.

"Difficult to tell in those seas. Three, four miles at the most. Just one boat, though."

Howard shivered, blowing through his hand for warmth. "Vladimir?"

"I can't tell."

They hoisted the big-boy sail in the rising wind, but it tore immediately and blew out at the head. Le Strange was called up from the galley to climb the mast for the wild free end of the halyard and for the remains of the sail attached to it.

Nelson ordered up the starcut spinnaker, but within minutes that, too, was tearing and he promptly had to get it down again.

"Okay," shouted Nelson urgently. "We can unreef the main and go up to a bigger genoa."

With the extra press of sail the Hood slammed more. She heaved into the waves with great shuddering crashes, as if she was shaking herself to bits inside. But she was sailing faster now.

"Bob!" Nelson clawed his way to the hatchway. "Can you climb the mast again?"

Le Strange held on, wedging himself against the violent slamming in the galley doorway. "Go up yourself!"

There was a brief silence of disbelief at this open defiance.

Then Keller rose to his feet. "I'll go."

They rigged the bosun's chair and hoisted Keller aloft, a dangerous operation at the best of times but particularly hazardous with the Hood driving and pitching on the backs of those enormous seas.

"I can't see anything!" shouted Keller. "It looks like we're in the clear!"

They crashed on in the gathering darkness. And snow fell again.

Nelson went below for his mug of soup. Sally, sipping hers, hands cupped round it, looked up guiltily.

What now? thought Nelson.

She saw the look on Nelson's face and looked down into her cup. "I'm sorry," she said. "I've heard it again."

"The radio?"

"Yes." She saw Nelson look at the empty radio room and Campbell in his bunk.

Nelson lowered his voice. "Was it before or after Keller joined us on deck?"

She shook her head. "I don't know. I was half asleep." She looked up. "Do you believe me? Or do you think I'm a fool?"

"I've heard it," he replied in a whisper. "But I'm not sure if it comes from on board or not."

"I think it must," she whispered. "I think it is Keller."

Nelson glanced at the hatchway to make sure that Keller, who had a habit of popping up to hear other people's conversations, was not listening. "Le Strange thinks so, too. He's quite violent about it." He was grim. "Wants to put Keller overboard."

She shrugged. "That's what we all think. Bob Le Strange. Me. Campbell. Pete Good."

"Don't be bloody preposterous!" retorted Nelson. "That's killing in cold blood. He'd never survive two minutes in this sea. Nothing is worth that!"

She faced him squarely, her voice rising. "Well, I'm telling you what we think. We can let him have the inflatable. It's got supplies. And a double bottom against the cold. He'd have a chance to live . . . even if he didn't get picked up by whoever it is that's breathing down our necks."

"You're getting brainwashed by Le Strange," he said scornfully. "What happens if we need the inflatable ourselves? If we get into difficulty? And what happens if Keller has to drift thousands of miles in this?" He pointed up and out of the boat. "He'd die before we got to New Zealand."

She took a deep breath. Slowly and quietly she replied, "That's his look-out. We didn't ask him on board. We don't want him on board now. We are fed up with having that Sword of Damocles hanging over our heads." She looked Nelson in the eye. "We are prepared to let him drown."

He stared at her quietly for a second or two. Then he lurched to his feet. "Well, I'm not."

The wind dropped in the night. The Shrieking Fifties no longer shrieked, although the Hood knew it was merely a temporary respite. The seas reduced at the same time to a rolling, heaving mass. They hoisted more sail and romped on.

Keller was lifted aloft in the bosun's chair for two hours despite the cold but he saw nothing except a couple of big white-marked killer whales a quarter of a mile off the stern. Again, at the thought of those whales, which had been known to sink yachts by attacking them and actually ramming through the hull, Nelson shuddered. If that happened to the Hood with Keller adrift in their liferaft there would be no chance for any of them. No good for them. Or for Keller. No, they couldn't set him adrift. Surely they must realise that? Anyway, he inclined to believe a lot of what Keller told him.

But that evening, with the wind howling again after the change of watch, Le Strange loomed over Nelson as he lay in his bunk. Le Strange shook him roughly.

"What do you want?" asked Nelson.

"I want you to sort that bastard out once and for all. I have heard that morse myself within this last half-hour. So have the others down here. Keller is in his bunk. Let us search him now. If he has a radio we will find it. Catch him red-handed. And if we do," he glowered at Nelson, "I will throw him overboard myself."

Before Nelson could move out of his bunk Le Strange was on his way, pulling himself hurriedly grab-rail by grab-rail aft to Keller's bunk. Geoff Howard followed him. Le Strange bundled Keller out of his bunk and held him while Howard delved through first the sleeping bag and then his canvas bag. Howard pulled out a small radio and held it up triumphantly.

Le Strange increased his hold on Keller, extracting a cry from him at the sudden pain. "You bastard! We'll show you what we're going to do with you." He struggled to get him towards the hatch but Nelson quickly moved up behind him and chopped Le Strange low down in the back, felling the big man with the one heavy blow. Keller dropped onto his bunk. Howard stood over him, holding the radio and looking first at Keller and then at Nelson with dislike. Le Strange pulled himself up glaring at Nelson but not making an attempt to go for him.

Nelson eyed him warily. "What have you got to say for

yourself?" he asked Keller.

"It is merely a transistor radio—an ordinary transistor that everyone has at home," said Keller disdainfully, rubbing his neck where Le Strange had hurt it.

"It's East German," said Howard.

"Of course it is," protested Keller. "I've come from East Berlin. Things are different there. Or haven't you heard?"

In a fury Le Strange grabbed the radio from Howard, angrily hoisted himself up into the cockpit and threw the radio far into the sea. He returned below and shouted at Keller: "If we can't get rid of you we can get rid of that!" He went into the galley. Howard glared at Keller with venom and went to his bunk. The Hood subsided into an uneasy truce.

Nelson gloomily moved away to wriggle into his oilskins. Keller did the same and followed Nelson out onto the deck. Campbell, at the helm, looked coldly away. Sally stared ahead. Tanner was lashing the retaining net back onto the cabin roof, which had been swept by solid water several times within the last half-hour.

Approaching in quick grabs, sliding his safety harness along the side safety lines, Nelson moved close to Tanner. "Where's Tooke?"

"On the foredeck."

"Wearing his lifeline?"

"Yes."

He watched with satisfaction as Tanner skilfully tied the lashing, no mean feat when his hands must have been numb with cold. "Any sign of icebergs?"

"No. But John's been keeping look-out. You'd better ask him."

Nelson's eyes tried to probe Tanner's wide red face. "Where do you stand? Are you like the rest as far as Keller's concerned?"

Tanner stood up, holding on tightly against the motion of the Hood. The two men, for a second, were stilled into silence. Then Tanner's grim visage melted a little. "I'm with you, Tom. Not because I have any sympathy with Keller or what he does but because, like you, I think it's insanity to think of doing anything else. What Le Strange wants is to go back to the Middle Ages. That's why I'm with you."

They were joined by Tooke, panting heavily after the wet effort to make his way aft. He glanced at Keller, who was watching them without emotion. "What do you make of him?"

Nelson wiped the spray from his face and licked the salt on his lips. "I reckon we can keep him on board, stave off the opposition and still win this race. Do you agree?"

Tooke slapped him wetly on the arm, smiling. "That's what I'm here for."

Nelson made his way back to the cockpit, where Sally sat uncomfortably on the gleaming slats of the side benches. "Won't you see sense?"

She did not answer.

"Leave her alone," threatened Campbell.

Nelson was surprised. "Pete, I need your support. I need your co-operation. How else can we see this race through?"

Campbell moved his gloved hands, swinging the wheel gently to meet the force of a wave. He nodded over to Keller. "Blame him. Since he's been on board we've hardly had a moment's peace. But I'll still do my job. You don't have to worry about that." He looked round at the sea with a look more like awe than fear. "I want to live. And if we can win, that's a bonus."

The following heaving day of iron grey brought the same friction, which heightened after they glimpsed a distant sail from the top of a huge roller. There was nothing they could do except to sail on with reefs in the main and a small jib, enough to cream them over the unrelenting sea at breathtaking speed. The wind howled at them but with no more power than they needed to drive them along and through those desolate waters as quickly as possible. During the day they glimpsed the other boat a couple more times but it aroused nothing more than growing bitterness against Keller.

It was cold. Snow fell. It froze on the windward side of the rigging, forming a crust of ice which, when the wind caught it, broke off and scattered in chunks. On deck it was a fight for survival against the pitching of the sea, the slush beneath their feet, the ice above their heads and the hollow sickness in the pits of their stomachs.

The wind rose. It moaned up, roaring through the stays and the mast and the ropes, whipping the sea into a boiling, maddened range of shifting peaks. The anemometer registered a force ten storm. They held on through the night and through the rest of the next day, while the elements smiled their contempt under a bright sun and a clear sky. The big southern seas curled back and struck at them, some of the waves sixty feet or more above their terrified heads, waiting for just one small mistake . . .

When the fleet had set off from England, the race rules

had been quite clear, even though they were long and complicated, aimed at safety for the competitors as much as the ease of the organisers; who were faced with the paralysing task of overseeing the longest, loneliest and most difficult race in the world. On top of minimum safety requirements of a high standard there was the matter of the course. The 27,000 mile contest had no fixed route except that a number of markers had to be passed and rounded. But, while the markers were laid down as off the Cape of Good Hope, between the north and south islands of New Zealand, off Cape Horn and off Florida, there was also a provision whereby the race committee could change the markers even while the contest was under way, on condition that there was a good enough reason to do so and always providing that they took every step possible to let the competing boats know.

And it was at this time, as the race committee surveyed the weather reports in a storm-swept club house in Auckland, and as they studied the latest ice reports, that they made a change which was to have a profound effect on everything that was to happen. Watching the weather with one eye, they cocked the other at the plots of the racing yachts. From the last radioed co-ordinates they put the Eagle and Vladimir, and possibly the Hood, in the lead to the south beyond the 55-degree line and level with *Der Rote Vogel*, which stormed on five degrees further north. Several hundred miles behind, in a loose area above and below the 87-mile island of Kerguelen, four yachts were fairly closely bunched. Behind them the fleet was scattered, only Italy making any impact on the race positions, sweeping forward with Latin élan now that they'd got everything together.

During the past couple of days the Hood had been driven on so quickly that she was between twenty and thirty miles ahead of whatever boat it was which had been in sight intermittently. That sail, the Eagle's, was also seen occasionally by the Russians, but the Vladimir was suffering now that two of the crew had been injured by a snapped spinnaker guy. She was struggling to keep up with the Americans. But fast as they were both travelling, the Hood was going faster, caught in a private storm of force eight winds, gusting to force ten. Her course was taking her clear of the northern limits of the ice and if she could only maintain her speed without foundering in the boiling seas she had the chance of building up a huge lead. Of course, anything could happen in such a long race, but it is certain that what the race committee decided at that moment would undermine everything that the Hood had done so far.

The committee decided that the New Zealand marker would be dropped from the race instructions. They sent out the message by radio and duly received acknowledgment from every yacht . . . except the Hood. It was a response which more than fulfilled the requirements of the rules and the New Zealand marker was erased.

But the Hood did not know.

Thirty-three days after passing the Cape of Good Hope, the Hood was alone, heading diagonally north from those latitudes of the deep, deep south up towards New Zealand, while the rest of the fleet dropped down towards the fifty- and sixty-degree lines. The Hood was quite alone.

Although the weather had quietened the tension had not subsided, but it was hidden and covered temporarily by the exhaustion of the constant fight against the cold southern sea and its snow, its hail, its fog and, above all, its howling, moaning wind. But the approach to New Zealand prised the feeling to the surface again, nurtured by the strange, ponderous thoughts of a crew which was seeing real land for the first time for nearly ten weeks. Then Nelson heard it coming . . . a long, low moan that came up fast like a line squall. It was a jet fighter, swooping low over them, only a few feet above the tip of the mast, and then whining on into the distance. The aircraft, trailing a dark line of exhaust against the white fluff of the sky, turned, rose and wheeled across the clouds to return the same way as it came.

Nelson sighed and steeled himself for whatever might happen.

On board the arguments raged for several hours while Keller, at the centre of the bitterness, gazed over the sea.

"If you want me to go," said Keller, "I'll leave you here while there's the chance. As you go between the north and south islands."

Nelson nodded glumly.

"Do you think we're ahead?" asked Keller.

The navy man shrugged. "Since Campbell gave up with the radio we haven't even been able to make a guess. But we've not seen a boat for days, so I should think we're up at the front somewhere." He glanced over at Keller. Coldly he murmured accusingly, "And since Bob Le Strange threw your radio overboard we haven't been troubled by morse transmissions."

But Keller remained unmoved. "You could just as

easily," he replied, "say that he has not been heard since Pete Campbell stopped playing with his own radio equipment."

"But you suffer one big disadvantage," said Nelson. "Nobody expects you to tell the truth."

Their conversation was interrupted by the distant thudding of a helicopter which grew from a dot over the far-off blue line of the New Zealand coast to the form of a New Zealand naval machine which circled the Hood in a welter of spray. It dropped a fluorescent pink buoy. On board the Hood some moments later, as the helicopter crew waved and turned back to land, the buoy was recovered and opened.

Nelson took a set of documents from inside. They were the revised sailing instructions. In silence he passed them down to Good. A desperate hush descended on the Hood as each, in turn, read the words and allowed them to sink in.

"That's that, then," said Campbell. The rest were too stunned to reply.

No word was spoken for, perhaps, five minutes. Then Nelson cleared his throat. "Get a new course, Pete. We're not finished yet." He pointed the Hood back towards the south.

Later, although they could not know it, their arrival back in the latitudes of the racing fleet inserted them amongst the trailing boats of the leading group—among the Saudis, the West Germans, the French and the Canadians—but, many miles apart, it would be a long, wild ride down the Shrieking Fifties before any real contact would be made between them.

Campbell, who had resumed his tinkering on the radio, claimed to have picked something up. "A bit fuzzy. But it was in Russian I think."

"Bloody good," said Tanner sarcastically. "That'll make everything clear."

"It's no problem," said Keller casually. "I speak Russian."

"Well, wadyaknow," said Le Strange with heavy irony. "Surprise, surprise."

"Cut that out," ordered Nelson. He turned to Campbell. "If you hear anything else call Keller immediately for a translation. I'd like to know but call him first."

A line of darkness approached from the north-west. The rigging began first to hum and then to moan that old sound of those lonely southern seas. They steeled themselves once more.

Again the Hood became a lurching, bucking monster on a boiling cauldron, driven on by a rag of a sail while the wind leapt to 70 knots. The storm jib, iron-taut in the immense howl of the wind, parted at the head and the Hood tossed under bare pole, heaving madly in the wild waves and the streaked grey murk.

It was the pattern of the following week. Gales. Massive seas. Spume and spray. Wet. Cold. Lurching misery. In the fear of the shrieking north-westerlies, they forgot . . .

And the Hood was swept down, down, down towards the icy wastes of the Antarctic; deep down, beyond fifty degrees south, beyond fifty-five, beyond sixty degrees, down towards the pack ice and on towards the big icebergs waiting for them in the desolation of the southern ocean.

At last a dawn, clear and metallic, opened on them without that fearsome moan of the wind. The sea—humped and heaving—galloped past with shining mane, but it was, at least for the moment, a sea of kindness, low and friendly under a steel blue sky. They romped on towards Cape Horn, two words which struck chill in their hearts. Cape Horn! The ultimate.

Nelson followed Sally to the forepeak in the dwindling light at the end of that day, a hard blue velvet sucking them all into its rich pile. "It's breathtaking, isn't it?" He did not expect a reply and he did not receive one.

She leant on the starboard rail. The night was falling fast by the time she eventually spoke. "Do you know what tomorrow is?"

"No."

"Christmas Day."

It was dark. Nelson was organising the last watch of the day, telling Tanner to keep a sharp look-out for bergs and small lumps of ice that would warn them of nearby icebergs. It was then that they heard it.

They froze in terror. It was a long, piercing human scream, a blood-curdling scream which scythed through the night to raise the hackles on their necks. The crew was quiet. The silence itself was eerie now.

And then it came again. A harsh, ghostly human cry which was so awful that it must be coming from a tormented soul of the dead.

The crew solidified in their terror, unmoving even in the heaving of the ocean. Again it came, that scream. A yell

from the undead, pulsing fear down their veins. It held in its
horrible grasp all the pain of every sailor who had gone
down, pressed into the southern ocean by the cruel gales
and the seething seas running before them and behind
them.

There was a sudden flash of light and a beam, a searchlight stabbing the darkness.

It came from the foredeck. Keller stood there with one of
their big, powerful rubber lamps. He swept the beam over
the water. It pierced the darkness with a light which no
longer seemed friendly, harbouring the evil of that sound
itself in its attempt to reveal it . . .

Two massive albatrosses, white and ghostly, faced each
other in the unreal light in some kind of courtship ritual,
their wings held up in a sharp vee. One of them let out the
curdling yell . . .

Until then, in those howling lonely latitudes, they had
almost forgotten.

Christmas brought little cheer. Blinking at them from starboard was the refraction of sunlight on ice. But there were
two cries—one from Good, keeping ice look-out on the
starboard shrouds, and the other from Tooke, on the bow.
"There they are!"

A couple of miles to port was a sight which stunned them
as readily as the albatrosses had silenced them with fear the
night before. The Eagle and the Vladimir. Nelson's heart
changed to stone. He looked first at the yachts and then at
the fringe of ice blocking their way south. In the distance
they could see the glint of icebergs.

"Not the place to get trapped by the opposition," said

Keller.

"We'll just have to do the best we can," replied Nelson, blowing on his cold hands. The red of Sally's oilskin burned from the foredeck. "Sally! You'd better come aft. Just in case."

She refused. "We're running into patchy ice, some of it in pretty big lumps. Hit one of them and we're in trouble."

Nelson lifted the binoculars in dismay. There were icebergs ahead all right. And some big ones at that. They stood ahead looming above the water, scattered across the sea like gigantic floating walls of glistening blue. Over to the right lay a continuous wall of white ice—the solid ice line spreading up from the Antarctic. The Eagle was trying to close in on a diagonal course. The Vladimir was keeping to the outside, perhaps less than a mile away, although further away than the Americans.

Campbell popped his head out of the hatchway. "More trouble. The Eagle has been transmitting again. Giving our position to somebody. I don't know who they're talking to but from the reply I should say it's a ship."

"Or a sub," interrupted Keller.

Nelson bit his lip. "And if the Yanks are on the air you can bet your sweet life that the Russians can hear them, too. If the Russians know that the Americans have a vessel in the area they're not going to sit back and do nothing. There's probably been a submarine shadowing us all the way round.

"We've all been hearing things." Sally glowered at Keller.

"Let's solve the problem here and now," snarled Le Strange. "Let them have Keller. First come, first served."

There was a low murmur of agreement.

Nelson raised his fist. "We leave Keller alone. We don't want—"

He was interrupted by Keller himself. Keller had his big knife raised in his right hand, a menacing figure leaning on the mast, to which he had moved unseen during their discussion. "I do not wish to use this knife," he said. "But I will use it . . . make no mistake. I have been contacting nobody. I told you—that radio was a domestic transistor. What possible reason could I have for keeping the Russians or the Americans on our tail?"

Sally looked anxiously across at the Eagle, which was sailing closer all the time to the Hood's track although it was clear she would be some way behind by the time she reached it. She glanced again at Keller. "I'm sure you could have some devious reason. Can't you see? We don't want you on board. The Americans are our allies. Why won't you take this chance and go with them—and get the Eagle and the Vladimir off our backs?"

"Because he can't," said Nelson. "He stays with us."

But he could see that the Americans were slowly—but surely—catching them. Once they drew close they would be able to take the wind from the Hood's sails and Keller would be at their mercy. Ahead, in addition to the big bergs of several miles in length and two or three hundred feet in height, lay an even bigger danger for a small yacht. Ice floes. They were scattered over the sea, heaving and rolling with the swell, some big, some small, amid hundreds of square miles of brash ice. It was a chill prospect. Any one of the millions of big chunks of ice, difficult to see and to avoid, would be big enough to hole the Hood . . . and possibly sink her. Nelson shivered. He peered over at the thickly packed ice to starboard and felt the trap opening up to swallow them. He looked at the full sails and glanced impatiently behind at the Eagle.

She was groping forward now at the Hood but although she could not quite catch her, Nelson was not satisfied. He had to get the Hood away . . . and upwind, away from the ice to starboard, away from the Eagle behind and, if he could manage it, away from the Vladimir hovering over to port in the distance like a bird of prey. Nelson remembered the luffing match off Africa between the Eagle and the Vladimir.

The Hood peeled off to port and the Eagle stuttered, caught by the surprise of the move. The Eagle heeled over with the press of her spinnaker which, only halfway down as she turned upwind, swallowed her speed with a broach. Nelson thrilled to the chase, eyeing the Vladimir, now ahead and waiting.

He had to get to windward of the Russians so that he had the advantage, but the Russians had guessed his intentions and had hardened up on the wind so that this could not happen. Behind them the Americans had untangled themselves and were chasing.

Nelson changed course again. Another good tack. The Russians, caught by surprise, took a little time to respond, unlike the efficient Americans, who tacked like lightning. Adrenalin flowed through Nelson, flushed with excitement and anxious now at the new hazard threatening the Hood. They were in the ice, thousands of loose slabs—melted remains of a disintegrated floe. Ahead were bigger chunks, into which they were heading fast. And then not far ahead of the bigger floes were the massive bergs—long flat-topped monsters sitting like fallen white tower blocks on the surface of the sea. The ice was knocking at the hull of the yacht with a constant rattle as she laid over to the thrust of the breeze. Nelson stationed Sally at the bow to keep watch on the water. She waved him on.

The Hood kept the other two yachts at bay, maintaining the distance between them skilfully even though she was now having to pick her way through the big floes bouncing deceptively lightly on the swell, seemingly innocuous but able to pierce the hull with merely a nonchalant nod of an icy white head. Sally urgently thrust her pointing hand first one way and then the next, directing Nelson in his weave through the treacherous floating field of white peril. The Eagle and Vladimir, themselves surrounded by ice, tiptoed behind them.

They crept on throughout the long day and the long evening in the falling wind, chilled by the sub-zero temperatures. By now the first big iceberg loomed ahead.

"How long do you think that berg is?" Nelson blinked at the ice glare.

Good looked along the sheer face of the ice cliff towering silent and ominous up from the sea. "Ten or fifteen miles I should think."

"You're the navigator. Which way do we go? Port? Or starboard." Nelson's grim face hardly showed through the ice goggles.

Good was silent for a time. "Turn to port and there's the Vladimir. Head to starboard and you might be heading into a blind alley. A cul-de-sac of ice. I don't really know what to say."

Nelson called ahead to Sally. "How far does the berg stretch to starboard?"

She shook her head.

"We'll go to starboard," said Nelson firmly. "If we get stuck we get stuck."

Le Strange peered out of the hatch. "What a merry bloody Christmas!"

Keller glared at him. "Peace and goodwill unto all men," he muttered.

Le Strange smiled coldly. "Yeah, that's right. Peace and goodwill. Even unto you. I've rustled up a meal of seasonal cheer and a bottle of vino. Come and get it." He looked over at Sally. "Come on. Even Nelson isn't blind enough not to see that berg."

Nelson steered the Hood to starboard followed by the Eagle. With satisfaction he saw the Vladimir turn the other way and head north. Alone at the helm he felt his spirit merge with those cold but beautiful wastes, with the glistening blue-white shapes of fantasy carved by the mocking hand of nature into the massive bulk of the gleaming iceberg. The tension was slipping away from him and no longer did he feel threatened by the close presence of the Eagle, less than a mile away. The sky was now a clear deep blue, reluctantly giving way to what he knew would be only a short period of cold, velvet darkness. Sally appeared in the cockpit, immediately catching his mood, not breaking the peace of his solitude until she had crept over to him. "It's beautiful, isn't it?"

He nodded, unspeaking.

"There's a meal below for you. Better grab it while it's warm. I'll take over."

Nelson put the first forkful of food into his mouth. Campbell drew a piece of paper from his flap pocket. "I think you ought to see this. Transmission from the Eagle. I'm sorry. I missed the beginning, but she'd obviously given our position."

Nelson unfolded the paper. The writing was neat, in capitals. HEAVY ICE SOUTH AND EAST. BERGS EAST. RENDEZVOUS SOON. BEFORE HORN.

"I didn't get any more. Too much static. But it looks as if the Yanks are going to meet somebody."

Nelson shrugged. "Heard anything from the Reds?"

Campbell shook his head.

It was night, a bright shining night now of moonlight and white sparkle on the ice, which they were skirting by sailing south. If the Americans held their course, even in this weak wind, they would soon be alongside, for the Hood could not bear away, baulked by the iceberg. There was no escape. The moon picked them out on the calm water like a searchlight, etching the white of the sails into the indigo night.

Howard took the helm, his big mittens shielding his hands from the biting cold.

"Keep sailing alongside the berg," said Nelson.

Howard nodded in silence.

The feeling of peace had gone. Nelson caught the tension again. It filled the air like an evil smell, pervading the very soul. Keller sensed it, too.

What Nelson feared most seemed to be happening. While the Hood made her way down the iceberg the Eagle was angled closer, catching up perceptibly. In this light wind there was nothing much he could do about it . . .

except to turn round and head into the clutches of the Vladimir to the north. The night would not last long. But while he cursed the moon for lighting up the Hood so much he sent out a prayer of sorts in gratitude. For a heavier wind and pitch black about him would have injected huge danger into this venture, with the iceberg to port, ice floes all around, pack ice to the south, the icefield further south . . . Isolated there, in the loneliest place on earth, the crew of the Hood felt small.

Nelson saw Sally shiver and for a brief moment he wanted her badly—but he felt the passion pass. He lifted his binoculars and swept them slowly over the icy landscape of the berg and over the moonlit sea, at the irresistible Eagle, sparkling in a white robe of sail, and at the deep void of the sky.

"I think we could be in for some dirty," he said, pointing south and east, where the sky and the stars were becoming fused with a tell-tale greyness. It was something he had been dreading.

Keller, too, was scanning the distance. "I've been following the line of that growler for a long time," he said. "I am sure that there's something different about the line of it, just down there." He pointed ahead to a section of ice in front of the big grey sky-smudge. "Can you see it? There."

Nelson squinted through the glasses. He handed them to Good, who peered at the iceberg for several minutes. "Yes, there's a break in the line."

"What do you think? Is it a space between two icebergs, or just an indentation in this one?"

Good slowly shook his head and raised the binoculars again. "I can't say. It could be either. If it's a dent in the

berg and we sail into it we'd be caught in a trap . . . with ice
only a few feet beneath the water.''

Nelson grimaced. "That could make it a bit too dangerous for us to take the chance, then. I was hoping that we
might turn into it and count on its being a gap between the
icebergs—a space to get through.''

He looked again at the weird shapes in the big ice-cliff to
port, to the huge flat-topped wall of solid ice spreading into
the south and then to the Eagle, gracefully and silently
stealing diagonally over the cold glinting water on a course
which would intersect their own. His optimism faded. He
turned to Keller. "I'm sorry, but if they do catch us I can't
endanger the Hood. Not down here. There's no chance of
rescue. I'll have to hand you over if it comes to it.''

Keller was quiet. "The inflatable?''

Nelson shook his head. He glanced with pity at the other
man. "Sorry, Keller, but that may yet have to be used by all
of us. I can't let you have it. Not for just one man. Anyway,
what would you do with it? There's nowhere to go.''

Keller appeared not to be listening. He fingered the
bulge of his belt in his protective suit. "What do you think
my chances are of getting off the Hood and onto that ice?''

The naval man shook his head again. "Even if you could
swim, the water would be too cold. It would kill you within
minutes—or sooner. In any case you'd never even get a
hand-hold on the ice. You wouldn't stand a chance in hell.''

Keller shrugged and brightened. "Well, that would
please the rest of your crew.''

Le Strange heard him. "Dead right, pal. They can have
you with pleasure.''

As they drifted along the sheer face of the iceberg they

watched the grey swirl grow nearer. The Eagle was approaching. The crews watched each other silently, barely a quarter of a mile separating them.

The snowstorm swept upon them, flying out of the southern sky in a horizontal rush of biting snow, a fine powdery dust which clung to them in an instant crust. Nelson called through the lashing wind to Good. "Did you get the bearing on that break in the ice before it closed in?"

Good nodded.

"Take me to it. It's our only chance to get away."

Good shook his head violently and struggled up to Nelson. "It's too dangerous!" he shouted. "I've already told you why! We'd never find our way in this blizzard, and what if it's a dead end? We'd smash to pieces."

Nelson shrugged aside the warning. He called to Keller, barely visible in the blinding snowstorm. "Get the two big lights. Keep one yourself. Give the other one to John. I want you on the bow and John on the port side. Shine the beams out."

The wind whirled round the edge of the invisible iceberg. They could hear the waves rushing on it, bursting and boiling against it nearby. While the two crewmen stabbed the spinning darkness with the strong searchlight beams, Nelson held the bucking yacht as close as he could to the heaving thunder of the iceberg, until the sound changed. He glanced questioningly at Good, wiping his goggles. Good raised his thumb. Nelson turned the yacht in towards the iceberg in a nightmare of pitching, rolling and deafening din, the Hood burying her nose into wild, bursting water and throwing up stinging sheets of spray. The mad chaos lasted too long. Nelson hung on to the wheel in dismay, searching the lashing snow for the signs of certain disaster.

And then it quietened. For a frightening second or two the swirl of the snow lessened to show in triumph the massive, towering walls of white heaving on either side, rolling murderously in the seas which roared their own triumph of surging, smashing waves. The beams revealed a solid web of ice closing round the Hood. Trapped in the black depths of the blizzard and the tumult of the turbulent sea, Nelson was struggling. The Hood was fighting to rid herself of this madman who had been lured into a whirlpool of frenzy. He battled to keep her away from the crashing, furious water pounding the ice a few yards away to port and then cascading over the bucking Hood. He fought to prevent her sliding away to starboard towards the fury of the nightmare sound over there . . . and still the Hood went on.

Nelson had no time to think or to contemplate their fate. They held on tightly while he took her on deeply, deeply into the crashing, heaving bedlam.

Then they were free. Free.

And somewhere behind, perhaps a long, long way around the treacherous ice, lay the Eagle.

Relieved and quiet, struck by the bare terror of the past few minutes, the crew clutched at the Hood lovingly as they battled on against the pitching sea and the crunching ice pouring across the face of the water, battering the sides of the yacht in hammer blows as she leant her shoulder to the challenge . . .

A grey dawn found the Hood alone. The wind veered

round to the stern and dropped. The sun reappeared. They swept on . . . less than two thousand miles from Cape Horn. But they could not be complacent. Twice during that day they struck floes. Nelson inspected the hull from the inside, finding that the repair which they had made earlier in the race had taken the full brunt of the second blow and had been damaged again. Water was seeping in, but it was a let-off. The leak, only one of many minor trickles which had developed over the weeks, was not serious; the only minor piece of good fortune for no glass fibre repair could be undertaken in those temperatures.

Le Strange was put onto the bilge pump. He pumped the water clear in sixty-five strokes.

SIX

The Hood powered across the southern ocean towards Cape Horn. In four days, embattled but not yet exhausted, she covered slightly more than a thousand miles.

Nevertheless the Hood—although she did not know it—was not in the lead. *Der Rote Vogel* was in front by over a hundred miles. Hood was now being broadcast by the race organisers as missing, a prospect which cheered the British crew, able for the time being at least to hide in that anonymity. Campbell squeezed from the ailing radio several moments of traffic between the Vladimir and a submarine operating between them and Cape Horn. He overheard the Eagle speaking to a ship of some kind and it appeared that the two countries were carrying out a systematic search, concentrating their efforts on the wide sweep of water lying to the west and north of Cape Horn, where the British ship, HMS Crouch, should be waiting in her rôle as the Horn marker. The fleet had to round her to the north and then sail east to round Cape Horn before completing the circle around the tip of South America. Then it was up the South Atlantic, leaving a last marker to starboard off Florida and then home . . . over the North Atlantic and home.

Home. It seemed a long way off.

Disaster struck next day. A wave knocked them down. Tanner found himself in the way of the spinnaker guy as the Hood lifted herself up. It curled round Tanner's waist and, like a boa constrictor, began first to squeeze him to death and then to cut him in two. His life was saved by Keller, who dived forward to cut through the rope with his knife. The sail was lost, but Tanner was saved. He was hauled below, barely conscious.

Then the morse transmission was heard again.

Nelson was on deck with Keller and Howard when Good appeared in the cockpit. He had heard it above the swish of the sea, above the boat noises. At the helm Sally shivered. She'd thought all that was in the past. Now here it was again.

But there was one happy man on board. Keller beamed triumphantly. "Perhaps," he said majestically, "this will now convince you all that whatever else I am I am not the one who is sending radio signals from this boat."

Campbell added a further sober note. "The Eagle has made another contact. With a submarine. It's on the way to Cape Horn. The captain's just told the Eagle that an air search will be made, starting tomorrow. They didn't say who they were searching for but I'm willing to hazard a guess that it's us."

"It is a big ocean," said Keller. "They may not find us."

Nelson's face darkened. "If there is someone on board the Hood who is transmitting messages they probably already know our rough position. That can be the only reason for doing it. In any case they'll be able to spot us soon enough—when we get to the marker at the Horn."

Howard shook his head sadly. "Everything's out of proportion, lost its perspective. I don't know about the rest of you but I am beginning to think we've been scaring ourselves silly over Keller. What if we are actually caught by either the Eagle or Vladimir? They're not going to harm us, are they? All they want is Keller. All right, we don't want them to get him but it might come to that. It's as simple as that. And would things be anything different if we're found by a submarine from either Russia or America? No, they'll just take off Keller and go, leave us in peace."

Nelson and Keller exchanged a glance. "Now we're getting more sensible," said Nelson. But he knew that Keller was a bigger prize than that. He had to try to stop him being taken.

Next day they saw vapour trails. The planes were high. On the Hood they craned their necks and shielded their eyes against the glare of the sun, but saw the aircraft only as minute glinting dots. The sight of the planes, even the recognition that they might possess sophisticated devices to make Hood's detection certain, did not diminish the growing optimism on board, for now they were only one day away from the marker ship to the north-west of Cape Horn . . . one day away from HMS Crouch . . . one day away from Keller's release if only they could get him aboard her . . . one day away from their own release.
Sally's heart fell when she saw. She called to Nelson, who was preparing himself for Keller's transfer to the Crouch, which had, to mounting excitement on board, been coming into focus, first as a hint in the far distance, then as a smudge, then as a discernible ship.

"What's the matter?" shouted Nelson from the bustle of the cabin.

She raised the binoculars for a second look. "That ship is not HMS Crouch. It's not HMS anything!"

Nelson rushed to the cockpit. Keller was by his side. Nelson took the glasses, and first he, then Keller, scanned the ship.

"Not the Crouch?" asked Keller in dismay.

"No," said Nelson. "Argentinian navy, I should say."

The chill of disappointment yet again ran through them, for they already knew that they were neither in the lead nor even in second place. Campbell had picked up a faint signal which told them that *Der Rote Vogel* was in the van of the fleet, about fifty miles ahead of France, who, in turn, were about a hundred miles ahead of the Hood, to Good's own estimate.

The Hood rounded the Argentinian marker ship in silence, waving to the men on board in a grim charade, and turned south-east. Later, in a lumpy but kind sea, they crowded the cockpit within two miles of the humped shape of Cape Horn. They watched silently in a sullen awe, each with a glass of champagne.

The moment gone, they continued on an easterly heading, planning to head to the east of Staten Island, which lay to the north-east of the Cape. The island lay off the mass of Tierra del Fuego, separated from del Fuego's Cape San Diego by a wild stretch of water called Le Maire Strait, a 16-mile wide channel whose dangerous tides and races moved quickly in the centre but even faster at the edges.

Sally and Keller stared across the water to the grey rolling seas on the port side. Tooke and Howard had stopped work on the foredeck to stare, leaving them at this moment immobile with just a scrap of mainsail up and nothing more.

Nelson followed Sally's gaze over to the distant snow-capped mountains of Staten, but it was not the wild beauty of that desolate place which was capturing the attention of the silent awe-struck crew. It was the sight of a massive hulk of bulbous metal sliding upwards out of the sea in a slow rise from the humped spray, the rounded dark curves of a submarine gradually taking its place on the moving face of the water. It was the moment they had all been dreading.

Nelson scratched back over some forgotten recesses of the mind, over long-forgotten ship recognition tests. "It's a Russian Victor class," he said. "A bit out of date, but it's got a nuclear reactor driving steam turbines. About 4000 tons. And we can't get away. She'll do about 26 knots on the surface—and over 30 knots submerged."

Keller's face fell. "Well, that's that, I suppose. I'd better go and get my kit together." He started to haul himself hand over hand from the coachroof back to the cabin.

"I shouldn't bother," called out Tooke. "Look over there, on the starboard bow."

In unison the Hood's crew turned their heads towards the starboard side ahead of them. Amazed they watched a second submarine rising upwards like a massive primaeval beast—about the same size, approaching three hundred feet.

"American, I think," said Nelson quietly.

Good confirmed it. "Sturgeon hunter-killer. Fast. Nuclear."

"That's torpedo, isn't it, like the Russians?"

Good nodded.

While they watched, Campbell approached from the hatchway. "There's a bit of confrontation going on," he said, looking out over the sea, where the American sub was slowly making her way towards the Russians. The approach was very slow, almost imperceptible, until about four hundred yards from the Russians, she hauled herself to a stop. The two submarines, iced with armed men gathering at action stations, faced each other.

Nelson told Campbell to get back to the radio.

Neither of the submarines moved, their automatic weapons, quite clearly in view from the Hood, trained on each other in a motionless play of armed poker.

Campbell shouted up. "The Russians are telling the Americans to go away. I won't tell you what the Yanks replied. It's getting a bit nasty."

Nelson surveyed the Hood and her sails in a fresh earnestness now that he saw the grey line of bad weather on its way. "This is our chance to get away from them." He ordered the sails to be hoisted. "We're going through the straits while those subs are sparring with each other. It'll be a rough ride, but if we stick close to shore with the wind that's coming up we'll fly through."

He pointed the Hood towards the straits.

The yacht, like a horse unleashed for the gallop, raised her nose and snorted at the surfing seas beginning to roll beneath her. She took off in a wild ride across the foam and the spume.

Glancing over to the submarines, themselves pitching in the rising sea despite their size, he saw that they still faced each other like two boxers out in the centre of the ring soon after the first bell.

Campbell appeared again. "Neither of them is going to give way."

"Good!" shouted Nelson. "Hold on to your hats. It's going to be a shaker!"

In the teeth of the squall they surged into Le Maire Strait, Nelson ignoring all the safety measures in the Admiralty Sailing Instructions. They had the tide with them, which kept the sea down for the first part of their roller-coasting, and they took advantage of the surging current close in to shore to fly northwards in the grey, howling storm.

"Keep away from Cape San Diego!" shouted Good, worried now. He had just put down the sailing instructions of the Admiralty, who advised small boats not to go closer to the cape than five miles. "If there's a tide rip there it can swamp us. The tide gets up to ten bloody knots!"

But in the wild excitement of the romping escape, Nelson laughed into the howl of the wind like a Steinhoff. "All the better," he cried, a gleam in his eye. "I'm going right inshore."

The frenzied bucking of the Hood took on an even wilder, more furious lurching. It was almost intolerable, a pitching which flung them from side to side and from back to front, throwing loose gear around the cabin and threatening anybody who let go even one hand from a hand-hold. Sally pushed herself across the bulk of Bob Tanner, lying injured but now uncomplaining in his tossing bunk. Even in his pain he smiled at this new assault. "You can get in here with me if you really want to," he smiled, wincing as the yacht heaved and crashed noisily through the seas outside.

She laughed, too, out of breath with the effort. "Don't you get any ideas, Bob Tanner," she replied. "I just don't want to pick up any more pieces of you from the floor." She held him down to stop him being flung out and he weakly raised his hand to stroke her hair.

"Thanks," he muttered. He hoped the squall would last for ever.

But it did not. Beyond the wild fury of the sea off Cape San Diego the deep-throated whine in the rigging began falling and the sea gradually changed from a tossing cauldron to a big swollen roll.

They were back in the South Atlantic.

Further south the submarine confrontation continued. The radio bore witness to the flat bargaining between the two captains, the men agreeing to withdraw together to separate points 600 miles east of Staten Island, monitoring each other's progress as they went. As long as each abided by this condition there would be no armed confrontation between them. Caught up in the words were fainter voices—military advisers back home. The radio was a seething bubble of activity for a time . . . and then, as the two submarines made their pact, the airways subsided once more to a pained silence.

"I don't think that's the last we shall hear of them," said Nelson quietly. "It sounds very much like the beginning of the race to me. They might not have said so much, but it's almost as if they've moved out to their starting blocks in the Atlantic before someone fires the start gun. Bang! They're off. With us as the prize."

They sailed up the Atlantic, holding a course to the west of the Falkland Islands and fulfilling the promise of over 300 miles a day for several days, swept along by immense storms which, back home, would have scared anybody into staying off the sea for ever.

But as they flew along, at last able to say goodbye to the roar of the Forties they had their problems—leaks, damage, failures . . . None of these set-backs, however, compared with the mystery and tension of the radio transmissions, a faint morse message which rang out irregularly, unintelligible and apparently emanating from within the Hood.

For once the latest race positions gave them no real cheer. *Der Rote Vogel* was still in the lead, as far ahead as she had been when they rounded the Horn. The French were second, not far ahead, and between them and South America. The Eagle and Vladimir were tied together in their perennial untrusting combat less than thirty miles behind. And the next loosely grouped trio of yachts—West Germany, Italy and Saudi Arabia, south-west of the Eagle and Vladimir—were hard on their heels. There was still a huge leg of over six thousand miles to go and the crew of the Hood were restless and uneasy. They waited for the constancy of the south-east trades, which should appear over their right shoulders to carry them up to the thin Doldrums belt on the equator. But as they waited they wrung their hands, perturbed by the constant attention which the submarines paid them . . . even though it was at a distance of several hundred miles. The Hood plunged onwards on a knife edge.

The radio heightened the tension with a fresh mystery, thin words warbling transparently through the fragile air:

"Discovery to Hood. Discovery to Hood. Acknowledged. Repeat acknowledged. Will rendezvous in forty-eight hours at the position you suggest . . ."

Nelson noted the position and afterwards plotted it on the chart. Sure enough, it was where they ought to be in two days' time, all things being equal.

Le Strange, who had been listening alongside Nelson, scratched his head. "There's an HMS Discovery in the Royal Navy."

Nelson nodded. "Yes, and it's stationed around this part of the world somewhere."

Keller was smiling. "A British ship. British—we've nothing to fear from the Discovery. A rendezvous with her would suit me very well."

Nelson shook his head. "I do not like it. Not one little bit. If one could put faith in the Discovery, why would it be cloak and dagger stuff?" He called Good to the chart table. Together they plotted a different course for themselves further out into the Atlantic to miss the rendezvous position given by the Discovery by two hundred miles.

"Trouble is," said Keller, "it takes us too damn close to those submarines."

Nelson shrugged. "That's a risk we must take."

A familiar air of gloom settled over the Hood, not lifted by a calculation that she had moved up into second place to the south-east of *Der Rote Vogel* and south-west of the estimated positions of the submarines.

Nelson peered up into the sunlit sky, following the wide graceful glide of a big albatross, whose long wings took it wheeling down almost to unity with the inexorable swell of the seas.

"Seems unreal," he murmured.

"Everything seems unreal nowadays," replied Sally softly, gloomily looking ahead to the horizon. "I wish I'd never come. I never imagined it would be like this."

Campbell, receiving stronger radio signals since arriving in the Atlantic, became the nervous fulcrum of the Hood. They reached the time of the projected appointment with the Discovery, meeting only the surge of the sea, magnified in the silence of their held breath. It was not until three hours later that the radio came to life, brief and puzzled. "Discovery to Hood. Discovery to Hood. Where are you? Rendezvous abandoned. Am moving on estimated course of Hood. Search will be cancelled in twelve hours if nothing seen of Hood. Bon voyage if you're listening."

But they did not linger on the words of the Discovery, for something else was happening on the radio as the last two sentences came through. It was another signal, super-imposing itself faintly in weak desperation.

It was *Der Rote Vogel*. Weak but insistent. "This is the Red Bird, sailing in Worldsail. My position is twenty-six degrees south twenty-nine degrees west. Mayday. Mayday. Am sinking. Boat holed. Mayday. Mayday."

The message was repeated a minute later. And then, after another interval, it was repeated again.

Another voice cut in. "La Bohème to Red Bird. We have received your distress call. Having passed it on to all shipping. Acknowledge please. Over."

Der Rote Vogel, masked by static crackling over the words, responded immediately . . . "Position twenty-six degrees south twenty-nine degrees west. Urgent. Boat has been holed by whales. Watertight bulkheads are not preventing us from sinking. We will remain afloat for estimated thirty minutes at present rate. Pumps not coping. Repeat, we will sink in thirty minutes. Over."

"Acknowledged, Red Bird. We are altering course to twenty-six degrees south twenty-nine degrees west. Hang on and wait for us. We will continue to broadcast Mayday on emergency wavelength. This will be our last message. Bon chance. A bientôt . . ."

Nelson shuddered. "Poor devils," he said quietly. "Killer whales have been a bigger dread to me than Cape Horn, even though it's a million to one chance against being attacked."

Keller was not downcast. "You don't have to worry about *Der Rote Vogel*. Steinhoff is one of the world's survivors. Even in a big rubber dinghy he'd still win this race if he had a sail to hoist. And I'd like to remind you," he continued, "of at least one heartening fact. We must now be in the lead."

He ignored the sudden indignation. "There's nothing we can do about it. We have our own problems with the Russians and the Americans waiting out there. No, you cannot escape the fact that we are now in the lead and that if the French go to the rescue of *Der Rote Vogel* we are not threatened by La Bohème any more. We can still win!"

His words were met by unrelenting gloom. Howard replied: "While you are still on board anything can happen. I'll believe it when I see good old Blighty looming up and we're there in front."

Sally nodded in agreement. "I'll believe it when I see it, too. The Hood is jinxed. I'm sure of it."

But the Hood was picking up the south-east trades. She

heeled to the latest surge of wind in her sails in the warming weather. She flew along, bustling on top of a busy sea which dropped behind in a heaving swell of white wash, holding tenuously to her crew, who grew tired under the constant strain. The strain mounted with each change of sail to meet the more fickle direction of the winds carrying them up to the equator, and it mounted as they heard the radio traffic between the Russians and the Americans. Campbell called Nelson to the radio three times in twenty-four hours. "The Russians are warning them off again," he said bleakly. "I haven't been able to get it all down as this damn thing is going haywire again. I knew it was too good to ask for much longer. But something's brewing."

"There will be!" interrupted Le Strange triumphantly. He loomed large in his red oilskins. "I am now going to perform a miracle, a feat of such magical proportions that I will be promoted to first mate." He had in his hands a long line of thick white nylon, his crossbow and several chunks of meat.

"What are you going to do?"

"Come and watch." Le Strange tied one of the big chunks of meat onto the end of the line. He inserted a bolt into the crossbow and threw the meat over the stern into the sea. "Do that—and you get sharks! And sharkmeat. I'm going to fish for the beasts. They'll come after that meat and whonk! I'll get them with my bow. It's as easy as that."

Nelson shook his head. "How do we get a shark on board?"

"Simple," replied Le Strange. "I have here another bolt, permanently attached to a line. I fire that at the dead shark and we haul it to the Hood. And Bob's your uncle."

"Ugh!" Sally shivered. "I didn't think you could eat sharks."

"When you're hungry and in need of protein you can eat anything," chuckled Le Strange. "The food is going down. And what'll replace it is beautiful shark steaks. It's something we might just get used to. Of course," he smiled again, "I could always try for an albatross or two."

The meat trailed behind the Hood for a couple of hours but it was left untouched. Nelson checked the bilge. Water was seeping in but there had been no increase in the flow. He pumped the bilge and checked the number of strokes it took to get the water out. No increase.

"How long before we make it back to England?" Nelson asked Good.

Good shrugged. "From here it should be about five weeks, but that depends on holding on to a decent breeze in these south-east trades, getting across the Doldrums quickly—shouldn't be difficult at this time of year when the belt's only about a hundred miles wide—and not getting held up off America. There shouldn't be any difficulty in grabbing a gale or two to get us back home across the North Atlantic."

Nelson turned to Campbell. "Anything happening on the air?"

Campbell swivelled round. "Something's going on, Tom, but I don't know what. I can't hear very clearly now." The reception faded badly, leaving them in ignorance.

Dawn rose on a black dorsal fin following the trailing meat. Le Strange took aim as soon as the shark surged at it. The bolt thudded home and he fired the second bolt, quickly and expertly. Attached to a strong nylon line, it, too, embedded itself into the leathery flanks of the shark, which thrashed for only a brief second before trailing heavy and limp.

"Good shooting," enthused Nelson.

Le Strange was smug with success. He began pulling the shark up to the Hood in a swirl of reddening water. Nelson leant over the stern with him, holding a boathook.

Campbell appeared behind him in the cockpit. "Tom, there's something happening."

Nelson was too intent. "Not now, Sparky. It can't be that important. There's nobody anywhere near us."

"Please yourself." Campbell returned to the radio. The reception was faint and patchy, etched with crackling static. He heard traffic passing between two Americans. One was asking for clearance.

Campbell heard the reply. "Okay, Fish One . . . Okay, Fish Two . . . Stand by . . . Vulture? Are you ready?"

"This is Vulture. Affirmative."

"Okay, Fish One, Fish Two, Vulture. Go. Go."

Campbell rose to tell Nelson but stopped himself. What was he going to say? It could be anything, particularly now they were moving up the Atlantic into radio range of countless ships. He resumed his seat, seeking further words in his headset.

In the cockpit there was a bloody, slippery mess. Le Strange, to Nelson's disgust, had cut up the shark and was throwing the dripping chunks back into the sea. "It'll attract more," he said. The meat splashed into the wash behind the plodding Hood, which was quietly gliding through the water, stirred by only a faint breeze. A swirl brought Le Strange to the stern with crossbow raised. "See? I told you they'd come."

Nelson turned. "I'll get a mop and clear up this mess." He skated forward to the other end of the cockpit to call to Sally to pass out the mop but was stopped by a quick movement above the water way out over the bow. A black dot hurtled over the surface of the sea towards them, quickly assuming the shape of a Phantom jet, passing close by in a banshee wail and a scud of exhaust, peeling off to its right, surging into the sky and banking round in a wide circle. Another black mark appeared, tore at them at high speed and flew past in a deafening crescendo of jet noise . . .

Campbell was struggling to hear . . . "Fish One to Vulture. Have made contact. Repeat. Have made contact. Co-ordinate four-five. Repeat. Co-ordinate four-five." The hiss of background noise changed. Another voice cut in. "This is Vulture. I acknowledge. Co-ordinate four-five. Over."

The scream of the two US Navy Phantoms, circling wide and low above them brought the whole of the crew of the Hood onto deck. But, as suddenly as they had come, the jets left, disappearing rapidly, their curling smudges of exhaust hanging in the moving air for a few seconds after they had vanished into the distance.

Campbell made his way aft, his progress followed with silent, gloomy anticipation as he approached Nelson. Nelson watched him come.

"That's what I was trying to tell you about," said Campbell. "At least, I now presume it was them. Fish One and Fish Two. I heard them over the radio." He glanced worriedly about him, quickly scanning the sea. "They were talking to someone called the Vulture. Probably the sub."

However, a few minutes later, high in the sky, slow and tiny, came another aircraft. It approached slowly and tantalisingly. Nelson looked up at it as it soared almost motionless high, high above them. "That must be Vulture. Not a submarine at all." They waited in silence for something to happen. Suddenly blobs dropped below the plane and fell downwards. Parachutes opened, eight of them, dropping neatly down, slowly, slowly and then slipping into the sea about a quarter of a mile away. The paras, sinister in black wet-suits and hoods, released themselves and climbed into a big inflatable dinghy which appeared violently on the low waves as it inflated. Nelson's voice was scarcely above a whisper. "Prepare for boarding party." He turned to Keller. "Wonder what they'll do with you."

The paras were all in the dinghy now, paddling in unison towards them, bobbing on the sea as they came. On the Hood nobody moved, mesmerised by the scene being enacted before them, helpless to act, resigned. The big grey inflatable came nearer, its eight occupants paddling silently, big men, powerful, their faces unmoving. It was about fifty yards away when two of the neoprene-suited men moved. Holding coils of rope attached to grapples they dropped into the water and began swimming towards the Hood, transferring the loose coils to their necks to enable them to sweep through the water with easy thrusts of their arms.

Sally let out a cry of shock. "The sharks!"

With horror they watched a dark dorsal fin slice through the water away from the frenzy of the feed at the stern of the Hood towards the nearer of the two swimming parachutists. A furious swirl split the water and he was snatched deep in a boil of white foam and blood. He vanished from the surface while the other man swam furiously forward. Le Strange, Nelson and Keller towered over him from the cockpit as the grapple swung upwards over the stern rail. The rope tightened as two sharks shot towards him and he lifted himself from the water in dripping, breathless haste. He grabbed the rail, ready to swing himself over, free of the slicing dorsal fin which surged past between the Hood and the dinghy.

Keller raced forward. He swung a big metal winch handle against the parachutist's hand and then crashed it at his face. The black shining form of the man slumped back into the water, where he was caught in a frenzy of white spume. Blood clouded the water.

In the same second that Keller moved, Nelson grabbed the crossbow, raised it to his eye and pulled the trigger. The bolt smashed through the air and into the dinghy. Nelson grabbed the second bolt from Le Strange, loaded and fired. He followed its snaking line as it struck home in the already spluttering rubber hull. Keller cut the line. The six men remaining in it threw themselves into the water and swam towards the Hood, through the bloody red water.

They never made it.

The Hood was helped on its way—away from the ghastly scene—by the shove of the south-east trades, which blew hot and cold to thrust her on up towards the equator. Campbell heard the Americans trying to make contact with the paras. Later, as the wind pushed them on, Campbell turned to Nelson. "They've assumed that those paras are in control of the Hood." He listened as the drawling voice radioed the rendezvous position—one hundred miles south of the Bermuda marker. The faint voice signed off in an optimistic monotone . . . "Don't be too long. The Reds are on your tail. Let's keep ahead while we're ahead. Okay, then. See you in Florida . . ."

SEVEN

By the time the Hood ran out of the south-east trade winds and into the sparkling warm sun further north she had regained her racing spirit. The last position check appeared to put them in the lead some way ahead of the Americans and Russians. The French were no longer in the race, having put into Rio de Janeiro with all but one of the crew of *Der Rote Vogel*. The missing man was Steinhoff, the one they'd thought was immortal. He had drowned in the battle with the attacking whales. Brilliant sailing had brought the Italians well up in the fleet, which lay straggled behind, scattered over a wide area of the South Atlantic.

Ahead of them lay the final long trials of the most fear-some race on earth—first the fickle treachery of these Doldrums, then the contrary north-east trades, blowing from the west coast of Africa diagonally down the Atlantic. After that the fleet had to head north-west into the mysterious Sargasso Sea region of the North Atlantic, leaving the sunwashed West Indies and then the Bahama Islands to port, making for the marker between Bermuda and Florida.

Here the boats would find renewed strength, sniffing the

wind for home, grabbing hold of the strong westerly gales if they could, for the romping ride across the Atlantic for England. And then across the finish line at Portsmouth.

The sight of Sally bronzing herself on the foredeck made Nelson edgy. She was lean and delicious, her small scrap of bikini barely nestling on the ample firmness of her breasts, her long legs disappearing tantalisingly into that white hint of cloth beneath her soft flat belly.

In the Doldrums the Hood sat, drifting round, sometimes through the full three hundred and sixty degrees of the compass, but under the searing sun it was not so bad.

Then the inevitable happened. First one sail was spotted on the distant horizon far to the south. Keller, from the bosun's chair at the masthead, saw a second.

They glanced upwards anxiously at their limp sails and prayed for a breeze. Anything. So long as it moved them on, away from their stubborn pursuers.

As if in answer, a gentle breeze settled on them, brushing them softly through the water to the music of a quiet gurgle along the waterline. It was not much, but it was enough to keep the twin wolves of the Eagle and the Vladimir at bay. They came no closer, becalmed by the very calm which had held the Hood trapped in its quiet web-like grasp a few hours earlier. They were gradually swallowed in the pitch black of night.

Next day the Hood was alone on the deserted ocean again. The yacht chuckled along in the morning light and heeled happily as the big genoa and the full main gathered up the wind in their petticoats to hurry the boat on to the Sargasso Sea . . . and the final marker.

That day, as the Hood danced on, sniffing the way home,

Campbell picked up a conversation between the Russian submarine and her control.

Keller interpreted. "The USSR sub is asking her control for permission to intercept us. How does that grab you?"

"How does it grab you?" replied Nelson. "They're after you, not us."

"Well, you'll be pleased to know that headquarters are now going to obtain a policy decision in the light of present circumstances. It seems," said Keller with relish, "that I am at the centre of a rather delicate international situation."

Nelson turned to Campbell. "You'd better keep tuned in to that wavelength. Keller, stay here just in case you're needed in a hurry."

But the day passed peacefully. It was, although they did not know it then, the last time of real peace they were to have.

Everything began happening at once.

Keller called Nelson. "Come on down quick!"

Nelson put on the headset, but Campbell removed it hastily. He turned a few knobs and brought the sound up so they could all hear. It was a drawling American with a stern monotone.

"This is the US Submarine Marigold to Russian Submarine Leningrad. This is the US Submarine Marigold to Russian Submarine Leningrad. Do you copy? Please acknowledge. Please acknowledge . . ."

Good, listening at the doorway, exhaled a long, low whistle. "Wow, they've brought in the big boys. Didn't know we were that important . . ."

The radio crackled again. "This is the United States Submarine Marigold to the Submarine Leningrad of the

Union of Soviet Socialist Republics. Acknowledge please."

The sound changed against heavy background noise. "This is Leningrad. We acknowledge—"

"I am the captain of the US Submarine Marigold," drawled the American voice. "I am instructed by the President of the United States of America to advise you to withdraw from the British yacht, Hood. Your position is being monitored at this moment by my crew and by two submarine vessels of my country. Failure to withdraw will result in those two submarines sinking you without further warning. Another vessel will arrest the yacht Vladimir."

There was a brief silence before the radio crackled its reply. "I am instructed to inform you that the captain of the Russian Submarine Leningrad cannot accept this inter-ference with his activities on the high sea or the threat of American piracy. Over."

The American monotone voice was unmoved. "This is the captain of the US Submarine Marigold speaking to the Russian Submarine Leningrad. I am not authorised to enter into any arguments with you. I am ordered to tell you that if you do not acknowledge that you will withdraw immediately you will be sunk. Please acknowledge."

Silence again. Nelson and Keller exchanged glances.

Then the Russians came back. "This is the Submarine Leningrad to US Submarine Marigold. I am instructed to make the strongest possible protest about this interference with my legitimate business on the international waters of the Atlantic Ocean. Over."

"Do you acknowledge immediate withdrawal?" per-sisted the captain of the Marigold.

Brief silence. A crackle. Silence again. Another series of background crackle. "Acknowledged. Immediate withdrawal taking place. Will you acknowledge please?"

The listeners on board the Hood breathed in relief as the Americans acknowledged. The iron curtain of tension fell away. Nelson whistled quietly through pursed lips and punched Keller gently on the arm in jubilation. "That was bloody close."

Nelson and Good moved away from the radio. "How are we doing now?" asked Nelson.

"We're up to ten degrees north," replied Good with some satisfaction. "The West Indies are coming up far over to port. We must be just about level with Trinidad. You won't see anything, though. The islands are a good thirty or forty miles off."

Into the night Nelson and Sally were alone in the cockpit. Their eyes met in a lingering, knowing glance.

"What about Le Strange?" he asked awkwardly.

She shivered. "He's an animal. I don't want to talk about him."

Feeling her body next to his like that, her bare breasts hard against him, Nelson was on fire. He kissed her and she returned the kiss with an open-mouthed passion which he could not match.

She drew back. "What's wrong?"

He shook his head. "There's nothing wrong," he whispered thickly. "Except I thought you hated me."

She chuckled. "You're blind, Tom Nelson. Blind." She drew herself up and they kissed. He clung to her warm flesh in a spasm he had not considered possible with Sally

Downes. He lost himself in her softness as they stood together at the helm surrounded by a darkness which they could almost run through their fingers . . .

Two days later the morning was punctuated by the sight of a small aircraft high above them and by a single message from the Eagle, which gave her position as only twenty miles behind. Campbell relayed the message on to them. "The Eagle has lost contact with the Vladimir."

Before nightfall another light aircraft dropped down above them, circled and flew off again.

"What do you think?" asked Good.

"Could be the Press," replied Nelson, betraying no anxiety. "The race is drawing to a close in many ways. We're a bit out of things without a radio transmitter working properly but there must be a lot of interest there." He nodded at the sea. "Out there in the real world. We're in the lead. I suppose we must be heroes."

Good said quietly, "Ten days should do it, with a following gale."

EIGHT

The radio was a curse. They had been cursing it for thousands of miles and they cursed it still. Cradled in the warmth of the airstream which cuddled the Caribbean and sweeping on towards the final marker, they heard, first, the American submarine trying to make contact with Force Vulture on board the Hood.

Then that night, in the solid darkness of those climes, the mysterious morse transmission which had dogged them halfway round the world was heard again. It pierced the hearts of those down below and it sent a shudder through Sally, who clung to Nelson in the cockpit.

"Did you hear that?" she whispered.

He nodded and looked up towards the foredeck, where a dim shape sat looking over the bow into the romantic night. "Did you hear that, John?"

Tooke's voice returned through the night air. "Yes."

Nelson handed Sally the helm and went below. "Did you hear it down here?"

The muttered in agreement. Keller, in the aft bunk, drew himself up onto his elbow. "Tom, it came from further forward."

Nelson looked from face to face . . . Howard . . . Le Strange . . . Tanner . . . Campbell . . . Good . . . None of the faces betrayed a thing. "All right," he said. "It's one of you." He stared from eye to eye as the men returned the stare in silence. "I say this to whichever one of you that it is. I don't know who you're contacting. Or why. But the rest of us don't give a shit. We are out to win this race and if we can do it with Keller on board we will. If we have to lose Keller we'll resist first. And if we find out who is using a radio on board you'll be torn apart before you leave this bloody ship—"

They passed close to the American submarine's rendez-vous position soon after dawn. For a couple of hours nothing happened but then a black shape rose from the ruffled sea.

"Here she comes," muttered Le Strange.

"And she's not alone," said Keller, pointing north-east, where they could see the approaching dot of a plane. The submarine rose until it sat on the surface, where it did nothing except display a few scurrying figures looking and watching. The aircraft—a small plane buzzing fast and urgently—came down low, swooping over the sub and then down over the Hood.

"What do you make of that?" asked Good.

Nelson shook his head. "I don't know. But it looks as if the sub doesn't know what to make of it, either. Look."

The submarine submerged fast as the aircraft banked round in a tight circle, staying with them for ten minutes, making a series of low passes, several figures waving down as they did so. Nelson could see cameras pointing from what was quite clearly a flying troop of Pressmen. But soon the plane waggled its wings, banked in a steep turn and flew off the same way it had come. The Hood waited for the inevitable resurfacing of the submarine. But it never happened.

And there, at last, on the horizon, was the final marker— a red-painted charter ship.

They were buzzed by two more planes before they reached the ship, on whose decks hundreds of people were waving. Nelson heard a few cheers. He waved back, smiling broadly.

They sailed past the ship, where a launch bearing the name GRISELDA was bobbing alongside. Nelson could see that a few figures were climbing down into it.

"Looks like we're going to have company," said Nelson, "Probably a few Press people. We're heroes. Do you realise that?"

Campbell called up: "A message from the Griselda. They say congratulations. The Eagle is now in sight on the horizon. And the Tribune is sending out Barry Glover for an interview with us."

Nelson beamed. "Did they mention the Vladimir?"

"No."

Keller came aft to the cockpit. "Tom," he said seriously, "this is our chance . . . for you to win the race and for me to get off and get home and leave you to it. I've caused you enough trouble. Now I think it's time to leave you and—"

He was interrupted by Tooke, who now sat on the slatted seats to starboard. Tooke looked at them both. He had a towel on his lap and a camera dangling from its permanent position around his neck. His voice rasped out drily: "Stay where you are, both of you." He lifted the towel to reveal a gun beneath it. "And I can use it," he said, beyond reality. He moved his eyes warily to Keller. "Sit down over there, slowly." Keller, surprised, sat down on the port side of the cockpit. Tooke turned to Nelson. "I don't want any trouble or somebody's going to get hurt. I'm sure you don't want that any more than I do. Just tell the rest to stay below for a moment."

Nelson did as he was told.

"Right," said Tooke, his face unmoving. "When the launch arrives tell it to stay off so that it doesn't ram us. Just answer whatever questions they ask you, but don't give any hints about trouble—past or present. Keep it nice and calm, about us winning the race and all that. Don't let them come near."

Nelson looked at him with venom. "What the hell are you up to, John?"

Tooke did not reply.

A few minutes later the small boat, with a complement of a helmsman, a photographer and Barry Glover—red-haired, thin, bespectacled and a famous journalist in Britain—came up from the stern quarter, close to the Hood's hull.

"Get on with it," snapped Tooke in a low voice.

Nelson waved them away. "Keep away from the hull, can you?" he shouted. "I don't want any accidents at this stage in the race, thanks." He smiled to show that he was still friendly despite the rebuff.

"Everything all right?" asked Glover, shouting through cupped hands. Nelson held up his thumb in triumph.

"We're determined to win," shouted Nelson. "The

boat's still in good trim, the crew's fit, except for Bob Tanner, who was injured in an accident in the South Atlantic. He's not too bad. We can do it!"

"Did you hear about the Vladimir?" came back the question.

"No. Where is she?"

"She's just gone. Disappeared. There's no trace of her anywhere—and we've been searching with planes and boats." Glover looked up smiling. "Yet another mystery for the Devil's Triangle!" He wrote something in his notebook. "Where's Sally Downes?"

"She's below, having a rest."

"Come on! Get her on deck with a big smile. We want a nice picture for Britain!"

Tooke was unshaken. "Tell her to come on deck."

Nelson called to her and she appeared, glancing in surprise at the trio in the cockpit, Tooke uncovering the gun trained on Nelson.

"Just keep calm and nobody'll get hurt," whispered Tooke. "Answer the questions, don't say one word that'll make him suspicious, and then stay on deck."

She smiled broadly and leant over the port rail waving at the camera.

"What's it been like cooped up with a crew of randy sailors round the world, Sally?"

Nelson sighed. Come on, come on, he thought impatiently. Get on with it and let's go.

Sally grinned.

"Any romance blossom on board?"

Nelson raised his eyes heavenwards.

She smiled. "I'm in love with Tom Nelson."

"Thanks!" shouted Glover and the launch turned in a white swirl of spray. "See you back at Portsmouth! Give 'em one in the eye for Britain." Griselda returned to the marker ship.

In silence they looked at Tooke. He dropped the towel, keeping the gun pointed towards Nelson, and ordered Sally to move over next to the navy man. He waved Keller aft and moved to the hatchway. He called below. "Everybody up on deck! One at a time. I want to see your hands. And I want to see them empty."

He waited until he heard agreement from below before he continued. "I have a gun trained on Tom and I will not hesitate to use it."

Nelson, Keller and Sally heard a murmur from below decks. Then Tooke dropped his bombshell. "If you are thinking of disarming me, or attempting to act against me, I have to explain that I am working for a member of the British Government and that my only interest is in acquiring certain information from Mr. Keller now that we are nearing England. I have no wish to harm him or any of you and I will not do so unless I am forced to. From now on you will all do as I say. I do not pretend to be able to skipper this yacht and I won't interfere with Tom sailing her, as long as there's no funny business. If you want to win the race, I've no quarrel with that. Okay? That sets the record straight. Now come on and get up on deck—one at a time."

They emerged unruffled . . . Good, Howard, Le Strange, Campbell . . .

Tooke sent Good and Howard to join the other three aft, and motioned Campbell and Le Strange to the side deck where he could see them. All this time Tooke remained quite friendly, smiling at them. "I know this comes as a bit of a shock for you, but this is reality, so you'd better get used to it. I repeat that my only interest is taking the information which Mr. Keller has . . . and nothing else. If he agrees to co-operate with me, nothing on board need change." He turned to each in turn. "Do you agree to co-operate?"

In turn they each nodded. Good shrugged. "It doesn't make much difference. We were prepared to hand Keller over to either the Russians or the Americans if we were forced to. Handing him over to Britain seems eminently sensible, although the way you're doing this, John, implies that all is not necessarily what it seems. Am I right?" Tooke did not answer, turning instead to Nelson.

Nelson, too, was sceptical. "I think that we should all be very careful before we get carried away by patriotism. Like Pete Good, I suspect that John is not acting in the national interest." He turned to Tooke. "You said you were working for a member of the Government. Who is it that you represent?"

Tooke did not answer, keeping his eyes coldly fixed on Nelson.

"Well," continued Nelson, unmoved, "Keller gave me his full story a long time ago and there's one British politician who could fare badly—very badly—once Keller's work is done and a few names are disclosed. I'm talking about John Crane."

Good looked grim. "That left-wing bastard! You might just as well be working for the bloody Russians, John. Crane is the next best thing to nationalised shit that we've got in Britain."

Tooke smiled his thin smile. "I'm saying nothing. I just want you to co-operate. You don't really have a lot of choice."

Nelson glanced up at the sails, pressed hard now by a stiffening breeze which would take them home all the more quickly. The white of the sail, brightly reflecting the glare of the sun, stood out starkly against the rich blue of the tropical sky. He felt a trickle of sweat dribble and run from his armpit down his flank. "You don't expect me to work with you, do you?"

Tooke grinned and lifted his gun towards Sally. "Yes." His smile broadened. "In fact, just to make sure that everyone on this yacht decides to give me their unstinting assistance, Commander Nelson and Sally Downes will join me below decks in the cabin. If anybody steps out of line, first Commander Nelson will lose his command in a sudden, dramatic way and if that doesn't cure things Sally will follow him. Do I make myself quite clear?" The coldness in his voice—a ruthlessness which nobody had before discerned in him—surprised them.

As he spoke, Le Strange laughed with mocking disdain at Nelson. He turned to Tooke. "Just tell me one thing. Are you doing this because of some political quirk of the heart or just for plain simple cash?"

Tooke hesitated. "Money. I am a simple uncomplicated mercenary."

Le Strange glanced once more towards Nelson, smiling at him evilly. "Then I'll help you, John. I am a simple mercenary, too. I'll help you for a third of what you're getting. I am, of course, assuming that you've got yourself a decent deal . . ."

Tooke's face remained unmoved. "Okay," he said blandly. "But if you double-cross me I'll kill you. You look after things on deck and I'll keep an eye on Nelson and Sally below. If you make a wrong move on deck I'll kill them instead. Now—we might as well get this boat sailing."

It was the turn of Nelson to smile. "You'll have to. You haven't got any choice. Look behind."

Tooke sent his gaze over Nelson's shoulder and into the clear distance of the horizon. He could see a white dot, barely discernible, but there, unmistakably. His face darkened.

"That's right," mocked Nelson. "It's the Yanks. Remove me from the deck and you don't stand a chance of getting back to England before they catch us. We lose the race. You lose Keller."

Tooke remained buoyant, speaking with bright confidence. "That's a chance I'll take. Bob—take over the deck. I'll look after the cabin. But first," he turned to Keller, "I want the documents which you have in your belt."

Keller procrastinated. "I haven't got a belt," he said. Le Strange bounced down from the side deck and found the belt inside the waistband of Keller's trousers. He undid it and placed it around his own waist while warily watching Tooke. "Just to make sure you don't double-deal me," he said.

Tooke shrugged. "Please yourself. You could easily double-deal me but I'm taking the risk. I stick to my word."

"Nevertheless I'll hang on to this, just for insurance," replied Le Strange. He looked at the sails and then at the white pimple on the far horizon. "Right then. Let's get on with it. There's money on the race now, so we're bloody-well going to win it."

Le Strange crooked his forefinger under Sally's chin. "Cheer up, love. He might even be as good as me in bed." He roared with laughter.

With the gun, Tooke waved Nelson and Sally below. As they disappeared through the hatchway he waved Keller to follow. "I want to be able to see you."

Tanner sat up in his bunk. "What the hell is going on?"

He listened grimly as they told him and then began to throw off his sleeping bag. Sharply Tooke waved him back.

The Atlantic took in a huge breath and then puffed out as hard as it could. A gale hardened from the west, heeling them over in a spuming rush as the iron-grey storm overtook them and sent them roaring on, rising and crashing to England on a huge sea streaked with wild foam. Even on that seething, howling mass they could see the Eagle gaining on them. It was a sight which no longer harboured any fear for Good, Campbell and Howard. At that moment, panting and sweating in their oilskins as they worked half-submerged in their harnesses on deck, they wished that the Eagle would catch the Hood, so that Tooke and Keller could be purged away. But there was no time to look behind for more than half a second, for on the deck of the Hood life was becoming desperate. Solid walls of water smashed against them and swept over them. Twice the three men were spilled against the guard rails at the limit of their life-lines, unable to resist the weight of solid water boiling over them.

"For god's sake," gasped Howard. "We'll have to get some of this sail down. Otherwise we'll go under for sure.

We can't keep this up."

Le Strange, water cascading over his head, smiled without fear. "We can hang on for a little longer yet!" The noise of the storm, solid sheets of water lashing horizontally over the surface, carried away his words, drowning them, along with the men on board, with spuming white foam.

Visibility was now down to a hundred yards, but the violence of the waves prevented them from seeing even that far. The Hood rose and plunged from crest to trough to crest to trough in a life-and-death switchback ride, flung this way and that, racked in agony.

The jib ripped into a few inches of sailcloth and snaking rope. Pete Good, half-drowned in the boiling flow of white water across the tilted deck, struggled to free the remains of the sail. That done, he lay exhausted for a brief second before the violence of the foredeck forced him to crawl hand over hand back to the relative safety of the cockpit. Le Strange clung to the wheel, concerned now that the Hood was being overpowered by the roaring gale after all.

Above the noise he shouted to Howard and Campbell. "Reef the main right down to the top batten!"

"We'll never manage it. We can barely hang on! We won't be able to work the reefing gear and hang on at the same time, you bloody fool. You've left it too late!"

Le Strange roared in anguish and fury. "Don't fucking argue! Get on with it! If you don't there's . . ." The end of his cry was lost in a surge of wind and water crashing over him. The cockpit filled with swirling water, solid stuff which crashed against their legs, threatening to knock them off balance as they clung for life to anything near to hand. It was frightening, although not serious. The washboards inserted into the hatchway slides prevented anything more than flying spray getting down below to swamp them. The water in the cockpit would eventually drain away through the self-draining pipes.

But Nelson, clinging with difficulty to the seat round the saloon table, was worried. He could see water flying in heavy dollops at the bow INSIDE the boat.

"I'll have to go take a look!" he shouted above the crashing din.

Tooke, his drawn face white with fear, did not argue, allowing Nelson to move forward to investigate in a heaving, tossing crawl towards the bow. Every inch meant hanging on to lurching grab rails.

Exhausted by even this small distance, Nelson returned. "The repair is breaking down," he said calmly. "The glass fibre is delaminating. Coming apart. It must have been soaking up water all the way round the world. The storm is too much for it—and it's beginning to break down the hull around the edge of the hole, too."

Clinging on to prevent herself being thrown over, Sally looked up, frightened. "How bad is it?"

Nelson shook his head. "I can't tell. It might give at any time. Then we'll have to pump for dear life. Or we'll go down."

Through the rest of the day and through most of the night the gale hammered down on them in maddened fury, beating against the hull, crashing over the decks, filling the cockpit time and again, sweeping over anybody not below. But the repair was holding.

As the noise dropped and the wild pitching of the Hood

began to subside, Tooke regained some of his shaken confidence, glaring at Nelson with new-found authority, reinforced with his outstretched gun. "Get on the pump," he snapped, enjoying the power. "Otherwise the water in the bilge will slow us down and we'll wallow. That's going to make us easy prey for the Americans, and we don't want that, do we?"

Stubbornly, Nelson refused.

That made Tooke angry. He raised the gun at Sally. "You'll do as I order you. Get the bilge pumped out."

Nelson stared him in the eye in defiance. "I'll not move an inch until you tell me a bit more about what you're up to. It *is* Crane you're working for, isn't it?"

Tooke returned Nelson's glare and decided against pulling the trigger. "All right. I suppose there's no real harm in your knowing. Yes, it's Crane."

Sneering, Nelson continued his questioning. "Tell me what I'm beginning to suspect. Was it you sending out radio signals?"

Tooke hesitated, then shrugged. "Yes, it was me." He held up the camera slung around his neck. "I've got some transmitting gear in two of my lenses."

"Who were you contacting?"

Tooke shouted in temper. "Shut up! Get to the pump!"

Nelson refused. "I want to know. If you don't tell me you can kill me . . . both of us. I'll not make a move until you speak." He sounded as though he meant it.

"Okay, okay. I was transmitting signals to the navy. The Discovery. The navy boys have been taking orders from Crane."

That shook Nelson. "Christ, but now I think about it,

he's in the Cabinet. He'd be able to pull a few powerful strings. What does Crane want with Keller's info? Nothing straight, I bet."

Tooke retained his air of stone. "I'm not interested in his motives," he hissed. "He's paying me and he's paying me well. While I'm in his pay, he's the boss."

His answer infuriated the exasperated Nelson. "But can't you see that this could affect the security of the West? Can't you see that Crane could undermine the defence of your own country if he gave this information away?"

A flicker of a smile crossed Tooke's face. "What Crane does he does for himself. Nobody else. Anyway, I told you. He's paying me big money."

Nelson began to rise. "All right, John. It's clear which way you're going. But tell me one more thing. Why contact the navy with your radio?"

"The arrangement was that we should get Keller off if he ended up on the Hood. But each time we fixed it up something cropped up to prevent it. As far as the navy is concerned, they think everybody on the Hood wants to hand Keller over to the authority of John Crane."

Shaking his head, Nelson moved to go up on deck. "Why should you anticipate that Keller would end up on board the Hood? You could never have known. That's impossible!"

Tooke waved the gun at Nelson. "That is something I can't tell you. Come on, have a go at the pump. We've still got to get home in one piece." He turned to Sally. "Any nonsense from you and you know what'll happen to him. All right?"

She nodded quietly.

Tooke followed Nelson on deck, to where the pump was built in, underneath one of the slatted seats. Nelson bent down to lift up the top, glancing aft as he did so. A couple of miles behind, romping along as fast as the Hood in the clearing murk, was the Eagle.

He chuckled at the irony of it all and set to work. It was hard, pumping. There was a lot of water in the yacht and it took several hundred strokes to get the level down. He cursed the decision to have only one big, manual pump on board instead of an electrical pump.

An hour later Nelson had to begin pumping again. Water was coming in fast.

"We can't slow down," Le Strange told Tooke. "If we don't keep on pumping they'll catch us." He flicked his thumb over to indicate the oppressive presence of the pursuing Eagle. "Don't they ever give up?"

"Perhaps they just want to win," smiled Good, winking at Nelson as the latter sweated at the pump.

Nelson gasped in exhaustion. "Come on, Sparky, you have a go!"

Instead of Campbell, Howard moved forward. "All right, I'll do it. You have a rest, Tom. Sparky wants to have a listen to his radio. He's beginning to pine for it."

Le Strange stopped him. "We don't need the radio any more. Leave it," said the big man, picking up the winch handle. Below, Sally watched in silent horror as Le Strange appeared and systematically set upon the radio equipment with the winch, smashing it with a series of heavy blows which reverberated through the Hood. Tanner looked glumly at the destruction and shook his head in sorrow.

The following night and day passed in frenzied urgency,

for slowly but inexorably the Eagle was inching closer. Campbell and Nelson were forced to alternate at the pump to keep down the water flowing in from the bow. "It's coming in even faster now," muttered Campbell.

Nelson nodded. "If we stop pumping, we'll founder, and they know it."

Indeed, they did know it. While Le Strange watched over the crew Tooke hauled Pete Good below to the chart table. "Tell me where we are now."

Good pointed. "The Azores are somewhere out in front and over to starboard."

Behind them the Eagle was breathing down their necks. Above them the sails were hard-filled with a westerly breeze, taking them surging on towards England, now only a few days off. In normal circumstances it would have been a time of excitement and elation, excitement at the thrill of the neck-and-neck race with the Eagle, elation at the lead which they were still holding . . .

But now? Nelson watched Sally sadly. "It ought to have been better than this. I'm sorry."

She leant across the table, ignoring the watching Tooke, and laid her hand over Nelson's. She did not have to speak.

Every hour they had to pump. Pump, pump, pump. Sweating, they pumped. Exhausted, they pumped. Heaving, they pumped. Pump, pump, pump. They gasped. They struggled. They tired. And still the water slurped in.

Good stood up, aching and exhausted, looking behind. Despite the leak, which was worsening all the time, the yacht had more than held her own against the assault of the Eagle. Good smiled to himself a little smile tinged with sadness, for although they were nearly home, still in the lead with the American boat falling behind a couple of miles, it could all have been so, so different . . .

Exhausted, his eyes blurred with effort, he slumped below. Sally appeared from the galley with a mug of soup. He was joined by Nelson, whose haggard face was creased in exhaustion and burnt effort. He, too, sat in the saloon in silence, not even glancing up to recognise the presence of Tooke. Nelson took his mug, wearily nodding his thanks to Sally, who stroked his neck briefly.

A brash shout came from the cockpit. "Everyone on deck! Come on! Major sail change!"

They struggled like zombies on to their feet. Good and Sally went up first, followed by Nelson and then Tooke, who remained a few feet behind. On orders from Le Strange they hoisted every ounce of canvas to grab all of the strong breeze.

The Hood burst into new life. But, dispirited, Nelson and Good dragged themselves back to the cockpit, where Tooke stepped out of the way to make room for them without giving them a chance to put him at disadvantage.

Le Strange saw a tangle in one of the halyards and called to Howard, but he met with rebellion. Instead of obeying, Howard sat down, drained of all energy, and Le Strange saw that for a moment he was spent. "All right," he muttered in disgust. "I'll clear it myself. Tom, get on with the pumping. We must be getting full of water by now." He glanced uneasily over his shoulder at the pursuing yacht.

Tooke was grim. As Nelson approached, he curled his lip to reinforce Le Strange's order. "Come on, get—"

He was cut with a cry.

He was spun round. The gun flew from his hand, landing at Nelson's feet. Tooke cried in pain, grasping his shoulder, which was spurting blood.

Nelson quickly picked up the gun, pushed Tooke onto the cockpit seat and turned to cover Le Strange. As he turned, his heart leapt. Tanner's beaming face gleamed from the hatchway, where he stood wielding Le Strange's crossbow. Keller went to Tooke, who was still screaming and gyrating in his agony from a crossbow bolt embedded in his upper arm.

"Better get him below. Get Sally to have a look at it," said Nelson, quickly in command again. "Le Strange! Come here and pump, you bastard, it's your turn!"

Le Strange glowered at him, hunched his shoulders and swore under his breath at this new turn of events. Good took the helm and brought the wind back into the faltering spinnaker. New hope sent the Hood surging, and Good surged with her. Howard grinned at Nelson.

By this time Sally had ripped the sleeve from Tooke's arm. The bolt was in too deep. "You'll have to wait until we get home for treatment. It should only be another couple of days."

Behind Tooke, Tanner was weakly pulling on his oilskins.

"You can't go up there," she said sternly. "You must stay in bed."

"Just try and stop me now," said Tanner, breathing hard with the effort of movement. He had to hold on for a moment or two to gain his balance. "I'm not staying down here while all this is going on."

As he hauled himself up into the cockpit, Le Strange was

still pumping, thrusting the pump handle up and down with an easy motion.

"It's getting worse," said Nelson anxiously. He glanced nervously over his shoulder. "I think they're gaining on us. If they catch us now, after all this, I think I'll shoot myself."

Tanner looked up at the sails. "Do you think she'll take another 'chute?"

"I doubt it," replied Nelson.

But the Eagle was closing. Keller was anxious now. He was still holding the belt which he had taken back from Le Strange a few moments earlier. The precious documents were still intact. He didn't want to lose them again. He threw them below to the safe hands of Sally before resuming his watch of the onward march of the American boat. "How far from England are we now?"

Good shrugged. "Three hundred miles, possibly. But that's to the Lizard. After that we've got to make it to Pompey."

While he spoke, Le Strange was grunting. He was getting tired. "How much longer?" he gasped. "How much longer do I have to keep doing this?"

Nelson glared at him without pity. "Till you drop."

The Eagle was less than a hundred yards away and had turned in towards the Hood, ready to blanket her, board her . . . Nelson looked back desperately.

"All right, Geoff, we'll do as Bob suggests and get another 'chute up. We'll have to try to beat the Eagle."

Within a minute, in their desperation, they hoisted a light spinnaker. But the Eagle was inching even closer. Moreover, the Americans seemed determined to rub it home, for as soon as the Hood hoisted her second spinnaker, the Eagle followed suit, hoisting the sail almost to the rhythm of Le Strange's pumping.

Nelson turned to the Eagle just as the Hood's sails dropped, snuffed out by the looming bulk of the fast-approaching Eagle and her big spread of canvas.

"Shit. Shit. Shit." Nelson watched helplessly as the bow of the Eagle loomed up. But then it happened. The Eagle slewed round away from the romping Hood, broaching heavily across the waves, mast dragged down sideways by the weight of uncontrolled wind in her two spinnakers.

Howard stood cheerfully on the foredeck. Nelson smiled. The big Eagle lay sprawling on the water, tripped up by her own excessive energy, staggering only slowly to her feet while the Hood sailed on away from her tormentor. One of the spinnakers—the blast reacher—was wrapped round the Eagle's mainsail in a vast tangle, slowing her to a limping crawl impeded further by a big mess of cat's-cradled sheets. She was immobilised.

Jubilantly, the Hood sped into the gathering night. It was a heavy, heaving, gasping night. They had to pump and pump and pump through it to stem the mounting tide flowing in from the damaged bow.

It was only then that Keller went to retrieve from Sally his belt and the documents. Sally regarded him anxiously. "Wouldn't it be better if Tom kept them for the moment? After all, if the Eagle does catch us and you're taken off, there's just a slim chance we can hang on to them safely. You should know by now you can rely on Tom Nelson." Dubiously, Keller stood in thought. For a moment he hesitated, but then agreed.

"Okay," he said. "We'll try it your way."

Soon after dawn, to the steady throbbing of the

pumping, they could feel the Hood slowing under the weight of water. A Nimrod appeared and flew over the yacht in welcome; but even now, as she limped past the flicker of the Portland Bill lighthouse off to the north, the fates which had treated them so rudely during the Worldsail spectacular were still conspiring to plot the downfall of the Hood. Sally waved at the RAF plane, which banked round in a long circle, but it was a gesture disguising the mounting desperation which they all shared—even Tanner, who was guarding Le Strange and Tooke in their bunks.

Keller looked up, totally worn out, from his pumping.

Howard wearily stepped forward to take his place, frantically fighting the water which was slowly but certainly swamping them and dragging them back. Sinking no longer held any animal terror for them, because they were so near to rescue, but what they did fear was that the race, apparently in their grasp, would slip away in the final gasp. For the Eagle was gliding up in the distance once more . . .

Within four hours, as they were turning up the Needles Channel in a dropping wind, the Eagle had her in her sights. But still, in quick turns, the men on the Hood pumped. The Hood sailed on, slower than the Eagle, but still moving. They passed Hurst Castle, desperate now, pumping, pumping, pumping, pumping like a frantic heartbeat. Nelson glanced round from the helm. The Eagle was probably little more than half a mile behind now . . . and gaining.

Sally watched a fleet of little boats approach, carrying the Press and god knew who else. "Oh please, please, don't let us lose now, oh please," she cried out. The men pumped, conscious now that the Hood had settled lower in the water, wallowing along like a bloated pig which had gutted itself in a feast of greed.

Still they pumped and still the Eagle marched up on them. Three hundred yards between them now and the finish line off Southsea beach was still a mile away. On Southsea front a huge mass of cars, began hooting. The fever was infectious. But the Hood was getting slower and slower.

Sally was in tears. "They're going to pass. Oh god, no!"

Howard pushed Nelson aside and pumped as if his life depended on it.

"There's nothing I can do about it," Nelson told Sally sadly as the finish drifted up ahead of them.

But there was still a breeze to give a glimmer of hope to the wallowing Hood. Keller now was heaving at the pump. Howard panted, almost sick with the effort. The Hood heeled to an extra puff of wind and approached the finish.

However, so did the Eagle, sensing the chance of victory after over 27,000 miles. She strode out now, creaming through the flat spread of water with a chuckle at her bow, only yards behind now and coming up fast, knocking off the distance between them with derisory ease. A cheer of impending victory welled up on the Eagle. The cannon for the winning boat boomed out to mark the finish of the longest race on earth, followed immediately by the gun for runner-up.

Nelson sank to his knees in exhaustion. Howard slumped over the starboard rail, holding back his vomit. Keller hung his head on his arms, kneeling, drained of any further movement . . .

NINE

Sally leapt for joy and clasped her hands round Nelson's neck. She kissed him hard on the lips. "We've done it! We've won!"

Nelson glanced over at the Eagle passing between them and the beach and smiled weakly. It must have been a matter of about five yards.

The Eagle's skipper, a short, tubby, clean-cut man, shouted urgently across the gap of water. "You look as if you're in a spot of trouble!" he called. "Do you want us to take anyone off?"

Keller grinned. Nelson shook his head and smiled. He muttered, "Not on your bloody life after all these months," and called back, "No thanks! We can manage!"

But he turned to the others, who had followed his orders and had already packed their scant gear. "Get all your bags and everything else you want to take home. Put it all on deck. We'll keep pumping but we're making water so fast I don't know if we'll make it."

A committee boat approached, shouting wild congratulations. A bewhiskered man shouted up, "Do you want a tow into the creek?"

"Yes! We're sinking fast!"

They steered the Hood into the creek reserved for the fleet at the Royal Navy's HMS Vernon, where a huge cheering crowd had gathered in welcome. The people parted to make way for an ambulance, for which the committee boat had radioed. Keller was still pumping furiously but the Hood was markedly lower in the water now as she moored behind the Eagle, already making fast.

"You can stop pumping now," said Nelson, with a sense of finality. He ordered all the gear to be thrown up onto the quayside, while Tooke, pale and shaken, was helped up a vertical iron ladder and then into the ambulance, followed by Tanner, who turned. "I'll see you tomorrow in the Pendragon for the celebration."

Nelson smiled happily and waved his consent.

Keller sneered at Le Strange, who was quietly zipping his anorak, friendless and alone. "What do we do with him?"

Nelson's grin dropped for a second. "Nothing. The world is full of men like Le Strange . . . mercenaries in the true sense of the word. But look at him now! I wouldn't trade us for him at this moment. Let him go. The dung heaps are full of Le Stranges. Losing one won't help much."

"They've got police in the ambulance to keep an eye on Tooke," said Keller.

Nelson nodded. "He's different in a way. He deserves anything he gets. HMS Vernon didn't waste any time, did they? A car will be coming to collect us at 0900 hours tomorrow to take us for a visit."

In his hotel room, Nelson grinned. Resting on top of his clothes was Keller's belt. He glanced up at Sally and smiled. She was undressing. He held up the belt. "I never thought we'd get that back in one piece."

She moved towards him, tanned and tasty, wearing only her pants, her slim body sliding like liquid through the room.

They fell back onto the bed in a wild climb up a cliff of passion, writhing rhythmically towards the heart-stopping moment for which Nelson had been waiting.

They made love until late evening.

Spent at last, they rested on the pillows, silently enmeshed in each other. Sally moved over and leant across him, her breasts touching his chest in a soft, tantalising embrace. She bent down and kissed him. "I love you. Believe me, I love you." A tinge of sadness seeped into her voice. "Will you promise me one thing?"

"If I can."

"Don't ever doubt me," she said, unsmiling now.

He protested. He pulled her down and rolled over, gently entering her once more in a slow rise to more groaning ecstasy. As they kissed and gasped afterwards, she opened her eyes. "Don't forget what I said."

They lay in utter peace. Until the phone rang by the side of the bed. Nelson turned to pick up the receiver. It was Keller.

"Can you see me now?"

"Does it have to be now?" asked Nelson, glancing across at Sally.

"Yes. And alone."

Nelson sighed. "All right. Give me a minute to dress.

Where shall I see you?"

"In the bar of the Royal Beach. Make it quick."

Nelson saw Keller standing by the bar.

"What'll you have?" asked Keller immediately.

"Scotch. What's the matter?"

Keller ordered the drink. "I've been trying to avoid the damned Press for the last two hours. Le Strange has sold his soul. He's spilled the whole story—bar nothing. I had to escape—and retrieve my documents from you. You understand?"

Nelson smiled. "Please yourself. We'll get them now."

TEN

In the morning, after a long ride which took them both in a maroon Rover 3500 to a mysterious building many miles from Portsmouth, Nelson and Keller stood before a big, wide desk. On the other side of it sat Admiral Cornelius Thwaite. Standing beside him was a figure in a black suit, a drab man with deep, loose bags beneath his apologetic eyes. His skin was so pale it seemed almost green, the colour drained even further by his black hair, eyebrows and small, thin moustache. He was tall and thin, wearing an amiable smile in contrast to Thwaite, whose face bore no goodwill. He was studying a pile of daily newspapers, all of them blazoning the Hood and her success across the front page. There were "exclusive" interviews with Le Strange in the tabloids . . .

Admiral Thwaite looked up sternly at Nelson. It was a minute before he spoke. "Would you mind repeating what you said just then?"

Nelson exhaled nervously, not relaxing his stiff stand to attention. "I said, sir, that when Keller and I got back to my hotel room we discovered that Miss Downes and all her belongings had gone. And so had the papers which Keller had brought with him from Berlin. I'm sorry, sir. I trusted Miss Downes implicitly. I made an error of judgment."

The admiral, as clean-cut and spotless as he was serious, contemplated a Press photograph of Nelson hugging Sally and lifted his gaze to Nelson.

"Yes, Commander Nelson, I can see that you, er, trusted Miss Downes implicitly. From what I've read in these newspapers it seems that you and she have been, er, a little more than friends of late. Perhaps, Commander, an error of judgment, as you say. Nevertheless, it's a bit incongruous, don't you think, Nelson, that although you can bring a small yacht more than 27,000 miles around the world and overcome a wealth of difficulties, you let yourself down by falling for the guile of a woman? Caught with your pants down, in the truest sense, I should imagine." He sniggered.

"Yes sir," replied Nelson gloomily.

"And what happened to the Hood?" asked the admiral in the same level voice.

As if you don't bloody know, thought Nelson. "She sank in HMS Vernon's creek, sir. Half an hour after we tied up. There was nothing we could do."

Admiral Thwaite tutted and smiled without humour. He turned to Keller. "Bit of a disappointment for you, too, Keller, eh? Sailing all the way round the world and then having your precious bits of paper stolen after you've made dry land again?"

Keller nodded.

Thwaite regarded them both before leaning back to speak to his companion. "What do you think, Michael? Do you think they've been squirming long enough?"

The tall, thin dark man grinned amiably in return. "I think so, Admiral."

Thwaite stood up and walked to the window. "You did not fail at all." He turned abruptly to meet their faces. "Without knowing it you have been taking part in a plan, albeit hurried and messy, to fool some of our 'friends' on the wrong side of the Continent; a plan which in all logic should never have been successful, which could have failed in a hundred different ways, but which you both, with a whole catalogue of chance and mischance, carried to a conclusion which we must assume is successful."

Nelson and Keller exchanged glances.

"Yes, it is true," continued Admiral Thwaite. "I'm sorry Keller but the information you have been guarding so zealously all the way around the world was mostly bogus. A decoy of sorts."

He stopped to allow that to sink in. Keller's face betrayed no emotion at all. The admiral chuckled. "It's a trick to match the wartime story of the Spy Who Never Was. A bit clever, but we ought never to have got away with it."

"I'm sorry to interrupt, sir," cut in Nelson, watching the man in the black suit. "But, with every respect, would you mind getting to the point?"

"I'm sorry. Of course," said Admiral Thwaite patronisingly. "The fact is that you, Keller, were carrying a list of names which had only a mixture of truth and fiction among them, all designed to confuse the other side. We made sure that both the Russians and East Germans thought that Keller's information was genuine and vital to them, and that we succeeded is displayed by the close attention paid to you by the Russian yacht, Vladimir, and at least one USSR submarine. I presume they did not escape your notice."

He allowed Nelson a laconic smile.

"Our idea was a simple one to start with, one that's been used before. Feed the enemy with a big mixture of fact and fiction and they don't know what to believe. It takes them longer to unravel everything and check out all the facts, right or wrong, than to obtain the information in the first place. What they can't check out they become deceived by. We had to try to do it because we were sure that they were getting close to some home truths. Isn't that correct, Michael? We needed a bit of time to close a few doors."

The man next to him nodded seriously. "It's all part of the game," he said, with his deep, fruity voice which belied his etiolated appearance. "The plan which Keller followed in order to board *Der Rote Vogel*—a rather novel way, don't you think, of escaping from East Germany—was leaked piecemeal through one or two feeders. We deliberately managed to delay the East German yacht's departure by intercepting the spinnakers she was waiting for and holding them back. That way we could ensure that Keller would not be able to get straight to England."

He turned to Keller. "Sorry, Keller. We selected you for the job partly because we knew that you'd fight to the death to protect your information—an essential ingredient of any plan to persuade the other side that the information is genuine—and partly because you couldn't swim. Once you got on the Hood you couldn't get off unless it was caught physically by the East Germans or the Russians, who both knew your real identity within a few days of getting out onto the open sea. We made sure they knew. It was a hundred per cent certainty that Steinhoff would never put back. He wanted to win—at all costs."

Keller interrupted him coldly. "How did you know that I'd get onto the Hood."

The admiral replied, "Sorry, but we have to explain a bit at a time. You could have, once you were out at sea, done one of two things. You could either stay on the Red Bird and therefore fall automatically into enemy hands with your information—which is what we wanted. Or, if you did get off the Red Bird, it was certain that you'd make for the British boat. But the beauty of the whole thing was its frailty . . ."

Back came the chortling, fruity voice, directed this time at Nelson. "That's where your delectable Miss Downes came in. We have known for a long time that she has been—what shall we say?—a bit over-friendly to the other side, so we decided to use her many talents to our own advantage. While we were making sure that Keller would be safely trapped on *Der Rote Vogel* at the beginning of the race, we also had to make sure that if he did get off and get onto the Hood there would be somebody on board who would have a damn good go at getting hold of his precious information and feed it back to the East over the Iron Curtain. We inserted Sally Downes deliberately into the crew list, complete with some orders which she believed to come from her other masters. We got her onto the Hood at the last minute without any difficulty. All a bit chancy, though."

Nelson remembered Sally's plea to him never to doubt her. He swallowed hard and stared ahead.

"Don't take it too badly, Nelson," said the admiral

quietly. "We expected her to go for Keller, not you. She must have had a real soft spot for you."

Nelson looked away. "What about the Vladimir? Did she suddenly just disappear—like all the stories in today's papers. All that Bermuda Triangle nonsense? Or was she helped on her way to the bottom by, er, us and our friends?"

Thwaite did not flicker an eyelash. "For once," he said, "I think you had better believe what you read in the newspapers. The Devil's Triangle is mysterious and evil. Boats often disappear there without any trace."

Keller shook his head in disbelief. "Tell me. What part did the Americans play in this peculiar charade? You know that they, as well as the Russians, chased us and tried to get me off. They even sent a team of parachutists to intercept us."

Admiral Thwaite shook his head curtly. "If I may say so, another error of judgment. The Americans were never trying to get you off. The Eagle was instructed to stick to the Vladimir as closely as she could, that's all, without prejudicing the Americans' chances in the race, to try to get the Reds to believe that there was a big effort to protect Keller. But all the time they were trying to win. They're big competitors, the Yanks. Bloody good sailors, don't you think?"

He hesitated, reading Nelson's anger. "You are going to ask me about those parachutists. Yes, a bloody mess that. And avoidable, too. Somebody on the American side thought that the Russian sub was a real threat. That somebody didn't know the whole story and sent the men to protect you. Nearly caused a nasty incident. Tragic.

Tragic."

Nelson grimaced. "Why didn't you tell me all this before we set off?"

The tall man interrupted. "Couldn't take the risk, old boy. Your reactions, all of you, had to be totally genuine for this to work. Nothing less will do for an operation of this kind."

Keller broke in, "Where did Tooke come into all this?"

The man shrugged. "I admit he was a surprise to us all. A bit of a joker in the pack, if you like . . . John Crane, who is one of the genuine names on Keller's list, must have nobbled Tooke at the last minute when he caught wind of an impending scandal involving him and a few NATO secrets. He found no difficulty in getting somebody on board at the last minute because you, Commander Nelson, had made it quite clear to Government officials that you thought the original crew was too small. Crane must have hoped that by grabbing Keller's information he could keep his own name out of any trouble and thus remain politically sound and in the Cabinet.

"If anybody had discovered Crane's dubious involvements, make no mistake about it, there would have been an enormous scandal. At the very least he would have lost his place in the Cabinet. At worst he could have brought down the present Government. Just to make sure that Mr. Le Strange doesn't talk too loudly we've slapped a D-Notice on the Press."

He was interrupted again by Admiral Thwaite. "As it is, everything has been done very discreetly. There will be an announcement later today that Mr. Crane has been advised by his doctor that he must curb his activities because of a heart condition, that consequently he will today be resigning his seat in the Cabinet and that he will not stand for Parliament at the next General Election—or ever again. Meanwhile your little Sally Downes is winging her way across Europe with the papers that we hope will lead our friends down some terribly long, dark alleyways. We couldn't have asked for more than that."

Nelson looked sadly down at his feet.

"Don't feel betrayed," said the admiral perkily. "Her work was always going to be more important than you could ever have been. We knew we could count on her to do her job well. You were just an accident in her way."

Nelson shrugged. "I feel a bit cheated, that's all."

The admiral, full of bonhomie, came round the desk to the drinks cabinet by Nelson's elbow, pulled out glasses and began to pour four stiff malt whiskies. He handed one to Nelson. "Stuff and nonsense, Nelson. You won, didn't you?" He lifted his glass. "Here's to the owl."